MW01273126

MAGIC IN THE BAY ISLANDS

Robert Hager

Cover Design By Brian Olson
AlphaGraphics Tacoma
www.alphagraphicstacoma.com

DEDICATION

To:

The Late Barbara Russell-Hager, a world class first mate. She could walk the walk and talk the talk. A true (10) in every way. She is sorely missed by me, and all who knew and loved her.

Blondie, I wish you fair winds and smooth sailing wherever you are. M.T.Y.L.T.T. Always R.H.

ACKNOWLEDGEMENTS

This book is a work of fiction, however like many fiction novels, it has it's beginning in truth. Much of the story follows the ship's log of the sailing yacht "MAGIC". The couple in the story are real people, to a point; then the story takes a "What if" turn. I hope you enjoy the story as a work of a fiction. R.H.

I would like to thank my wife, Gina Kim Hager, for making me want to finish this novel I started some time ago but left unfinished. Her gentle push to have me finish this story convinced me to do so. Thank you Gina.

Also thanks to my friends for helpful input and assistance. Janice Dawson, Susan Kim, Kara Wages, and Jong Kim. I am grateful to Gene Davis for rush, rush, computer upgrades and assistance whenever needed.

CHAPTER 1

FRENCH HARBOR, ROATAN, BAY ISLANDS OF
HONDURAS

The moonlight glimmered off the evil-looking
machete lying at the feet of the dark-skinned native
paddling quietly towards the yacht Magic. The barefoot
man, clad in old blue jeans and black T-shirt, was in the
process of carrying out the tradition of his ancestors.
Born from a long line of Spanish pirates and escaped
slaves off the mainland, this islander was a busy man.
His cayuco, a hollowed-out log, rode low in the water
due to the stolen merchandise that filled it to the
gunwale.

Pulling alongside the sixty-five foot world class
motorsailer, he reached up and tied a line to the stern
rail. Though the yacht was moored to the dock in front
of Romeo's Steak and Seafood restaurant, he knew the
security guards were seldom awake during the early
morning hours. Plus, he had other reasons not to feel
threatened by the security force. Feeling confident, his
tall slender frame, strong from much paddling, swung
expertly over the railing. Passing a locker, he noticed a
pocketknife lying on top. That might come in handy, he
thought, claiming it as his first prize. Moving
noiselessly, he quickly reached the cockpit. His dark

eyes, experienced at working in the moonlight, began searching for objects worthy of his collection.

Something startled the native and the pocketknife fell to the floor. The clatter was a shotgun blast in the quiet harbor. He froze. In the main cabin, a dog began barking. Since being chewed by a Doberman during a midnight shopping spree, the man was terrified at the prospect of reliving the experience. His bare feet climbed up out of the cockpit and quietly ran toward the bow of the yacht to hide. He saw the beam of light sweeping the deck. He crouched behind a large locker bolted to the foredeck and waited.

#

JIM AND TOBI SHAW ABOARD THEIR YACHT MAGIC IN ROATAN, HONDURAS

After a difficult eastern trip with high winds on our nose from Livingston, Guatemala, to the Bay Islands of Honduras, my wife Tobi and I had cleared customs uneventfully in Coxen Hole, the capital of the island. Our destination was Roatan, the largest island of the chain just off the eastern coast of the small Central American country. We had finally arrived in French Harbor in Roatan. At the invitation of the owner of Romeo's, a popular restaurant, I had guided Magic to the dock area in front of the restaurant.

Jose Romeo had regaled us that night with tales of piracy and shipwrecks in the area, but he assured us that with his security force on the job we didn't have anything to worry about. After an evening ashore filled with delicious food and palate-pleasing wine, we were more than ready for bed around midnight. Since it was much easier to get a good night's sleep in the center of the yacht than in the bow, we usually slept across from each other in the main salon bunks rather than in the master bedroom.

Weary from our travels, we welcomed the familiar comfort of the bunks and sank into a deep sleep. Sometime during the night, Tobi dreamed that Jim was licking her face. Coming out of a light slumber, she realized that Coco, our faithful Pomeranian companion, had climbed onto her bunk and was giving her a tongue-bath. "Okay, Okay," she said. Assuming Coco wanted to go outside, Tobi started to swing her long shapely legs off the bed when she heard a loud noise in the adjacent pilot-house area. Peanut, our small ferocious poodle, started growling. This gave Coco the signal to leap to the floor and begin barking. Tobi looked over to her sleeping husband. "Honey, Honey, wake up." Her voice conveyed more urgency than usual.

Startled, I awoke. Disoriented from perhaps too much wine and too little sleep, I took in the commotion around me. "What's going on? What time is it?"

Tobi whispered hoarsely. "Someone's on the boat."

I sat up and began clearing the cobwebs from my head while Peanut and Coco continued their duet.

"Jim, wake up. Someone is aboard the boat."

"Okay, okay," I said, stumbling out of my bunk in my skivvies. Grabbing the five-cell flashlight from the shelf over the port-side berth, I climbed the three steps leading up to the pilot house. The screen door leading to the outside cockpit and steering station stood open. Now fully alert, I was sure that the screen had been locked. As I touched it, I could see where the mesh had been cut by a sharp object. Someone had reached in and lifted the hook securing the door. Stepping into the cockpit, I shone my flashlight around and located my Old Timer pocketknife lying on the deck. I always left it on top of the flag locker in the pilot house. I swept the light around the harbor and toward Romeo's. The night was deathly quiet.

My skin began crawling as I stepped up from the cockpit to the main deck on the starboard side. Seeing two hand held Icom VHF radios tossed carelessly on the deck, I wondered if the intruder had already carted off more than he could carry. Carefully working my way forward, I realized that whoever might be on board could be armed. I thought of my wife and canine friends and became worried for their safety.

Angrily, I flicked the light around, seeing nothing. Approaching a large white fiberglass storage locker on the bow, I became tense. The eight by four foot locker, used to store mooring lines, diving gear, and other bulky items, was a likely hiding spot. Cautiously making my way around, I reached the midway point of the locker.

My heart stopping, reflexes took over as I swung a downward arc with my five-cell flashlight at the head of the intruder. The hard swing connected and the shadowy figure fell backwards, tumbling over the lifelines into the pitch black waters of the harbor.

Realizing that pieces of flashlight and batteries had slid along and off the deck after the stranger, I concluded that I had lost a damn good flashlight. I bent over the lifelines and peered into the dark water. Hearing a noise to my left, I swung around, prepared to take on another attacker. Just in time, I realized it was Tobi scurrying along the deck with her nightdress flying out behind her and a stainless-steel Smith and Wesson 9mm semi-automatic pistol secured in one hand.

"Did you see anyone?" she asked, trying to catch her breath.

"So far one guy jumped out from behind that locker and I knocked him in the head with my flashlight. He fell overboard," I said, looking down into the water.

"I would have been here sooner, but I wanted to lock the puppies in the bathroom so they wouldn't get in the way."

"Well, I don't see him," I said, turning back to Tobi.

"Do you think you killed him?"

"I hit him pretty hard. He might have drowned."

"Are you sure he was by himself?" She asked, looking around with the semi-automatic tight in her grip.

"Slow down, Kid. I think he was alone, but we'll turn on the spreader lights and have a look around."

"Here, take this," she said poking the pistol at me, "before I accidently shoot someone."

Taking the pistol, I put an arm around my wife. "Just calm down. I think we caught him before he got into too much mischief." Walking back along the deck in silence, we both stayed alert for any unusual noises. Tobi stepped down into the cockpit and hit the switch for the spreader lights. The large lights mounted high on the spreader arms of the main mast illuminated the entire area around the boat.

"Look what we have here," I said, grabbing a line tied to the stern rail and pulling the native cayuco toward the yacht.

"Jesus, that can't be all from our boat." She exhaled as she looked over my shoulder at all the merchandise piled in the dugout.

"I don't think so, but get me a pair of shorts. I'll climb down and hand this stuff up, so we can see what's ours."

Tobi brought me a pair of cut-offs that passed for my boating shorts, and I slipped them on. Laying my pistol on the deck, I went over the stern rail into the cayuco. Tobi leaned over the rail and took the items from me as I lifted them up. After two small TVs, three VCRs, two medium-sized brown suitcases, and a large box of cassette tapes and videos, I laid my hand on the native's machete. Holding it up in the light, I could see that it was over three feet long and razor sharp. I was grateful the intruder had left this baby in his boat. I hated to imagine holding off someone carrying this weapon with my now defunct flashlight. Instead of the native falling overboard with a dented skull, I could have ended up with pieces of myself scattered over the bow.

Shuddering, I threw the monstrosity into the water. This finished, I asked Tobi to untie the dugout's line from the stern rail. This would allow me to pull the cayuco over to Romeo's dock. Climbing up the ladder off the dock, I stood looking down at the bounty. Deciding that the prowler might return, I began heaving and shoving until I pulled the dugout from the water and onto the dock.

Returning to Magic, I watched Tobi picking through the box of tapes. With all the items piled on deck, the place resembled a flea market. "Jim, I've never seen any of this before. It's not ours."

"You're right. It doesn't belong to us," I agreed.

"Where do you think it came from?" she asked.

"Well, I doubt if it belonged to our visitor. We were probably last in line on this dude's work schedule."

We were still sorting through the loot, making small talk like two nervous kids, when three local men came from around Romeo's restaurant and onto the dock. I reached down and rested my hand on the 9mm. Two of the men wore security guard uniforms with sidearms attached to their belts. The third, in jeans and T-shirt, wore a white rag, serving as a bandage, around his head. Their expressions intensified their already dark faces.

"Captain, this man tells me you have some of his belongings on your boat," said the older security guard, who appeared to be in charge.

"I doubt that." I said, kneeling with one knee on deck.

The wounded man spoke. "That's my stuff, man. It ain't yours."

"You're right it's not mine. But it's not yours."

"You took that stuff from my boat," he said pointing to the dugout on the dock.

"You're right, but if you want it, you need to contact the police."

"So, you're going to rob me, just like that," the bandit said', getting closer to the railing of the yacht.

I stood from my kneeling position, gun in hand. "Don't come any closer."

"Captain, I'm in authority here," the older guard said, with his hand on his buttoned pistol holster. If you have a problem with this man, you'll have to work it out with me."

"That's not the way I see it. I'd rather settle with the local authorities or Romeo. I'm here at his invite. In the meantime, head out now and take that thief with you," I said', pointing the pistol towards the outlaw. "And, if you value your jobs, I suggest you call the police. I know your boss very well."

Troubled, the three men stood looking at each other. Nate, the older security guard, spoke in whispers to them. The other security guard was more than ready to leave, but the would-be-pirate glared at Jim threateningly.

"If you don't give me my fuckin stuff, I'll return with my machine gun and waste your Yankee ass," the man said, waving a fist for my benefit.

Looking at the wet bandaged desperado, his chest puffed out with indignation, I didn't take much stock in his threats. He didn't look dangerous. "Run along and do what you think best. But be careful, because I promise to be ready for you."

"Fuck you, man," the thief said, and started towards the cayuco.

"Leave it on the dock till morning," I yelled harshly.

The thief ignored my command and pushed the dugout into the water much more easily than I had taken it out. I let him go. Soon the native had sculled the dugout around Magic and paddled up the bay until he passed the first canal and was gone.

#

The two security guards turned and quickly walked away, talking as they went.

"Sir, you don't think the thief will come back for blood, do you?"

"I hope not," the guard sighed, shaking his head in frustration.

CHAPTER 2

After our visitors' departure, Tobi and I were alone aboard Magic and the bay area was peaceful again.

"You think he'll come back?" she asked.

"I doubt it," I answered.

"What if he really does have a machine gun?"

"He didn't look like he could afford a machine gun. Remembering the machete, I added, "Just in case, I'll stay on watch while you get some sleep below."

"I could stay up here with you. I won't be able to sleep anyway."

"No, Baby. I need to turn the lights off and stay hidden in case he does return. Try to get some sleep."

"I'll try," she said reluctantly. "But you be sure and call me if you hear something. You might need my help. Promise?"

"Okay, I promise."

She leaned over and pecked me on the lips, then went below. I watched her long firm body leaving and thought how lucky I was to have her.

A retired pilot for the airlines, I had spent twenty years of hard work and saving before my wife and I managed to buy land in the Rio Dulce Valley on Lago De Izabal, Guatemala, a large fresh-water lake with access to the Caribbean by way of the Rio Dulce River to Livingston, Guatemala.

We fell in love with the area at first sight. Being boat bums at heart, our new home was the ideal place to keep our sailboat, Magic, with easy access to the Atlantic Ocean. So for six months a year, I ran the farm, named La Dulce Vida—"the sweet life" in Spanish. I did crop dusting for nearby banana plantations and occasional contract flying for the CIA. This left six months to pursue our passions: sailing, diving, and looking for underwater treasure.

This year, we planned our trip to coincide with the rainy season. Late summer and fall we had decided to explore the Bay Islands of Honduras and do some diving around the old pirate strongholds in and around Roatan Island. We were especially intrigued by the infamous Port Royal Harbor, along with other numerous bays and cays with colorful pasts dotting the Bay Islands. There were many tales of sunken treasure to be had. After purchasing a cruising guide and gathering as much historical information as we could absorb, we set sail for Roatan Island.

I wondered if I had been right to take the native lightly. I was stout enough at taller than six feet and heavier than two hundred pounds, and though I was over fifty, I still retained much of my strength from my power-lifting days. But it's hard to wrestle a machine gun. Even I didn't want to wrestle a three-foot machete unless I was forced into it.

Checking my weapon for a round in the chamber, I pushed the safety switch to the on position. After extinguishing the lights, I searched for a watch point on the bow of the yacht. I settled on the area where the brass hawser holes passed through the hull. The hull extended eighteen inches above the deck for added free bound and mooring lines to pass through. Positioning myself flat on my stomach, I could look through one of port side hawser holes with a good view of the bay in front of the boat and of the canal entrance where the cayuco had vanished.

After a long hour of the gentle rocking of the boat with no activity, I was just about to doze off when the patter of little paws brought me to attention. Coco jumped in the middle of my back and passed over searching for a place to take care of business. I could hear Tobi following close behind.

"Coco, come here."

She playfully stepped on my back also, and then hustled Coco back to take the puppies ashore for a moment. I decided not to stop her. I was still alert when she came back later and lay beside me.

"I couldn't sleep and the dogs wanted out. So I thought I would say hello and see how you were doing."

"Honey, you shouldn't be up here."

"Come on, I'll just stay a minute."

I couldn't argue much with my wife pressed up against me. In her early forties, she was still built like a swimsuit model. Wearing a thin nightgown, she diverted my mind from the task of watching for pirates. I rolled to one side and put my hand behind her blond head and held her tightly squeezed to me.

Tobi looked up as the luminous moonlight revealed the silhouette of a small boat passing the canal and turning in our direction. She froze. Leaning over she whispered, "Jim, someone's out there."

Grabbing my face with her long fingers, she said urgently, "He's out there." She watched the dugout get close as I found my Smith and Wesson. The strong native form was sculling his way, slowly and silently, toward the yacht. Grateful that the dogs had been quiet up to now, I motioned for her to gather them up and she crept back aft.

I watched the native approaching fifty yards off the bow on the port side, close to the area where I lay concealed behind the hull and cap rail. Finally, the wait was over. The native, bent on revenge, brought his small cayuco alongside and stood up to grab the cap rail on the hull to steady himself and keep his cayuco from bumping the hull of the yacht.

When the intruder's hand settled on the cap rail, I tensed in a squatting position, placing my left hand over the intruder's. Holding the pirate's hand to the rail, I placed the semi-automatic to the native's nose in one swift motion. It was the intruder's turn to freeze.

"Please, don't move," I said in a calm voice, struggling to hide my nervousness. "I don't want to blow your head off—unless I have to," I added.

Startled, the intruder could only gasp. He remained still. "Just the slightest movement and you'll probably lose that face of yours." He received the message loud and clear. I leaned close and looked the visitor over carefully. Sure enough, it was the VCR pirate, but with a smaller bandage affixed to his forehead.

Pressing the pistol firmly to the man's head, I looked over his shoulder down into the dugout, and between the visitor's spread feet there lay a MAC-10 machine gun, complete with what appeared to be a thirty-round clip in place. Feeling the hair rise on the back of my neck for the second time that night, I considered pulling the trigger.

"I want you to reach down with your right hand and take the gun by the barrel. Then lay it here on deck. Remember, if you are not very careful in your movements, I'll probably blow your head off."

Very cautiously, the native bent to one side and grasped the MAC-10 by the barrel. He lifted it over the rail and laid it on the deck next to me. The metallic sound of the gun striking the teak deck brought Tobi scampering from her hiding place where she had been watching the action.

"Oh, my God. He did have a machine gun," she exclaimed, staring at the fearsome weapon lying on the deck next to her husband. "I just knew he was serious about killing us."

"Take it easy, Kid. This guy's had a bad night. Besides losing all his loot, he just lost a damn good machine gun."

I considered my options as our visitor continued looking up the barrel of the Smith and Wesson. "Tobi, would you pick up our friend's weapon here by the barrel, please, and carry it back to the cockpit. Lay it down very carefully, and wait there for me."

"My God! You're not going to kill him, are you?"

"I don't know. But please, just do as I ask. Okay?"

"All right," she answered reluctantly. Picking up the MAC-10 like a poisonous snake, she went along the deck towards the stern of the boat.

As I focused on my nervous black friend, I was missing out on a beautiful sunrise. The sky began to lighten along the horizon, promising daylight. It would be several hours before the restaurant opened. I couldn't take the chance of holding the man at gunpoint until then. I didn't have the slightest idea where the police station was located, so I couldn't send my wife ashore for the police. After my earlier encounter with the security guards, I didn't trust them. If the guard let the thief loose again, next time he might bring friends. As I attempted to reach a decision, the native stood motionless without making a sound.

Suddenly, distracted by a noise behind me, I had the decision made for me. The bandit bolted backwards into the water. Caught off guard, I fired reflexively at the fleeing target. I was sure that I had connected, but the pirate continued swimming. I was a competent enough shot to easily end the native's career. I aimed the pistol at the moving target and began to slowly squeeze the trigger.

"Jim, no!"

Lowering the semi-automatic, I turned to see my wife staring at me like a sheep-killing dog—a look that says, you know better. "Okay, Kid." While the intruder swam to safety, Tobi came to me. Setting the 9mm on the white storage locker, I put my arms around her and held her tight.

"I'm sorry," she said. "I wasn't thinking. I should have let you shoot." She trembled in my arms. "Now he'll probably come back."

"It's all right, It's better this way. I couldn't stay watching him forever until the restaurant opened. In a couple of hours, I'll go over and call the police. Hopefully, they'll be of a better stripe than the security guards."

"Do you think they'll catch him?"

"This island isn't very big. They can find him if they try."

"I'm beginning to get tired, but I'm not going back to bed. No matter what you say. I'm staying with you. I can hear better than you and you might need my help."

I couldn't argue against her logic. After spending forty thousand hours piloting various aircraft, the noise had taken its toll on my hearing. Hating to wear the two inner canal hearing aids, I had learned to read lips while in the process of losing my hearing. "Okay, but you'd better let the dogs out of the bathroom."

"They're probably tired of me locking them up."

I eyed her attire. "You might dress a little more conservative in case we have more company. I mean, you look great to me and our visitor probably thought so too, but . . ."

She smiled. Still sporting a filmy nightgown, there was no doubt she could stop traffic.

I continued to stare. "Maybe after some coffee, we'll kick back out here on the aft deck and get something started."

"Don't be making any promises unless you plan on delivering," she said with a wink.

"Cross my heart," I said and watched her disappear through the cabin hatchway.

CHAPTER 3

We waited until the restaurant began showing signs of life. Exhausted, we sat lounging on the aft deck with the two tireless canines, checking our surroundings. One hundred and fifty yards away we could see where the cut led into a picturesque harbor. The sea could be heard breaking on both sides of the rocky entrance, with lighted buoys marking safe water. We could see the wreckage where a fiberglass trawler had missed the cut during rough weather. Jose had told us that the captain had tried his luck with one of the channel lights burned out. With the keel broken, it appeared to be a total loss.

By looking over the pilot house toward Magic's bow, we could see the Hyatt Company shipping dock, where processed shrimp and lobster were shipped all over the world. South of the Hyatt, the Sylvester dry dock handled the majority of the paint and repair for the area's lobster boats. Directly across from us, located at the far end of the bay, stood Albert Jackson's. Being the largest store and marine supply on the island, it handled the fuel and ice for the work boats, along with anything a tourist or resident might need to survive on a small island. The rugged hills rising from behind the Jackson complex were breath-taking from the distance. Though they were only five hundred feet above sea level, they looked much taller because of their location on the water. Watching the early morning sun and mist rising from the hills, Tobi and I almost forgot the trauma we had experienced during our first night in the harbor.

By the time we began hearing noises coming from the restaurant, we were both getting drowsy from lack of sleep and the calming effect of our peaceful surroundings.

"Well, I better get started before I fall asleep. If you'll fix breakfast, I'll step ashore and see if I can get someone to call Jose Romeo. I'd hate to get involved with the police before I get some advice. Especially with the report of a stolen machine gun report. I might be the one that ends up in jail. Or worse."

"That's a good idea. I don't know if our lawyers could help much over here."

I stretched the cramps from my legs while Tobi started to round up breakfast. Taking the 9mm, I turned to Tobi in the cabin passageway. "I'm going to leave this on top of the flag locker while I'm gone."

She looked at me apprehensively. "Just hurry back."

"I'll hurry," I answered. Stepping over to the dock, I walked toward the restaurant. The large double doors opened onto the dock area during business hours. Definitely not a breakfast-type restaurant, the heavy oak doors were locked tight. I could hear movement inside so I knocked and waited. A few minutes later, one door was opened by the biggest, blackest woman that I had ever seen. My six foot three and two hundred twenty pounds were dwarfed next to this gal. Her face radiated good humor with a big smile. She wore a large red bandanna turban-like on her head and necklaces with half a dozen strings of colorful shells and beads with like decoration at each wrist. Covering her huge body was a multicolor fabric sewn into a sack-like dress with enough material for sails on Magic.

"Morning, Captain. I'm Ruthie. Hope you and the misses are enjoying our island. Somphin I can do for you?"

"Good morning to you, Ma'am. I was wondering if you could call Mr. Romeo for me."

"Lands sakes, we don't have no phone, but we got a radio. I could try to get him for you."

"That'd be fine."

"Well, come on in, Captain, and I'll turn on the radio. It's got to warm up, you know. But it should be ready in ten minutes. Could I get you and the misses some coffee or somphin while you wait?"

"Thank you, I could use some coffee, but my wife is getting breakfast ready on the boat."

Twenty minutes later, she had Jose on the radio. She handed me the mike.

"Jose, this is Jim Shaw on Magic. Could you come down to the restaurant as soon as it's convenient?"

"Is there a problem?" The radio crackled.

"Nothing that can't wait till you get here. Just need some advice on something that might interest you."

"Be down in half an hour, if that's okay."

"Fine, thanks. We'll be on the yacht. See you then."

"I appreciate your help, Ruthie."

"Don't mention it, Captain. Anytime."

Stepping aboard Magic, I started into the cabin when Tobi met me at the hatchway with the pistol in her hand.

"You scared me," she said, laying the gun back on the flag locker.

"Sorry, I should of hollered first. Oh, by the way. We got company coming. Jose Romeo said he'd be here in thirty minutes."

We entered the pilot house. There was bacon and eggs along with toast and fruit on the table. Tobi poured juice and turned to me. "I was getting worried about you. I thought our nocturnal friend had sacked you over there."

"No, it just takes a while to get hold of people around here."

We had just finished breakfast when we heard Jose hail us from the dock. "Permission to come aboard," he shouted.

Stepping up to the cockpit, I answered, "Please, come aboard, Jose. I'm sorry I had to call you so early, but after I explain, you'll understand."

Jose greeted us and I offered him a seat at the dinette table in the pilot house and began the tale of the previous night's events. Jose was quiet and didn't interrupt until I finished my story. "Don't worry about the security guards. They won't be working here anymore. I'm just glad you called me before the police got involved. Let me take a look at the items you took from this guy."

It took a few minutes for us to cart everything from the main cabin to the pilot house. After examining the video cassettes, Jose was surprised to see a familiar name on one of the labels.

"Damn. This is one of my wife's tapes."

"Did you get robbed?" Tobi asked.

"I don't think so, but I better go over to the restaurant and get her on the radio to be sure."

While he was gone, I noticed the name Maria Romeo was written on several of the videos and cassettes. When Jose returned, I showed him the additional tapes that belonged to his wife.

"Well, at least he wasn't in my house. Maria loaned the tapes to Betty Sylvester. Her husband, Paco, owns the dry dock across the harbor. The other property probably belongs to them. Maria went to get them and bring them here if it was their house that was hit."

"What about the police?" Tobi asked.

"If you don't mind, let's hold off on the police for a while. Around here, the police confiscate property as stolen, and then it really is stolen, because you'll never get it back."

"That's fine by me. You live here and I would rather you deal with the police if you don't mind," I said.

"Sure, I'd be glad to."

While we waited for Maria, Jose filled us in on some of the history of the bay and of the island. I was fascinated with the stories of pirates and sunken treasure. I asked Jose about old Port Royal, and Jose agreed that there were probably several ship wrecks in that area. Tobi and I exchanged glances.

An hour later, though the time seemed to fly by, Maria appeared with the Sylvesters in tow. After introductions were made, with some input from Jose, I recapped the events of the previous evening. The three newcomers seemed suitably impressed with the near capture of one of the local villains. Going through the loot, the Sylvesters claimed all the stolen merchandise.

Paco said, "You did me a big favor by not reporting the MAC-10. The authorities frown on those a lot here, even though several people have them." Then he asked, "You didn't by any chance see six hand grenades with this stuff, did you?"

Tobi looked like she was going to faint. "Hand grenades! My God! He could have blown all of us up."

I was feeling uneasy, but tried to be confident. "Well, I didn't and he might not even have them."

"Yes, but you're the same husband who didn't think he had a machine gun either."

"You're right," I admitted. Looking at Jose, I said, "I really think we should have the police, or someone, round this guy up. We have to sleep sometime, and I hate to think of him on the loose."

After a few minutes' discussion, Jose agreed to collar his security guards and find out who the fellow was.

"He may be the nephew of the guard. We've had trouble in the past with a man called Carlos Soto," Jose told us.

"If it was him, you're lucky his partner was busy somewhere or you would have really had a problem," Paco Sylvester replied.

The Sylvesters gathered their belongings while everyone agreed to meet at the restaurant around two that afternoon.

"As soon as I speak with my security guards, I'll have the police find and lock this guy up."

"We'd appreciate it," Tobi said quickly.

After all our company went ashore, Tobi and I decided to take a much needed nap. I thought about making good on my promise of hanky panky, but looking over at Tobi, I saw she was fast asleep with a dog on each side. Before having a chance to consider much else, I followed their example and passed out from exhaustion.

Much later, Tobi shook me carefully. The pistol was on a ledge next to my head. With all the excitement, she wasn't sure how I would awake.

"Jim, wake up," she said.

"Is he back?" I said, sitting up.

"No. but we have to be over at the restaurant in thirty minutes."

Once again, Peanut and Coco had to go into the "dreaded" bathroom.

The Sylvesters had been waiting a while by the time we walked into Romeo's. When the owners arrived, the four of us were having a beer at one of the tables.

"Mission accomplished," Jose said, taking a seat next to Tobi." It *was* Carlos Soto. His uncle, Nate, denied it, but the other security guard confirmed that it was Carlos. I fired Nate on the spot, but I told the other guard I'd give him another chance."

"Is Carlos Soto dangerous?" Tobi asked.

"He's just the local pot connection, but we've suspected him of other things for quite a while," Paco Sylvester broke in.

"This is the first time anyone has caught him doing anything," Jose added. "The police found him hiding at his mother's house on the other side of the island at Anthony's Point. They have him in custody, so you can sleep safely tonight."

"That's a big relief," I said.

"He'll be safely locked away until the magistrate arrives and sends him to the mainland for trial," Jose explained.

"I feel better already," Tobi replied gratefully.

"What about Zep?" Betty asked. Jose and Paco looked uneasily at each other.

"Who's Zep?" I asked. I was getting a bad feeling.

Jose spoke up. "Zep is Carlos's partner."

"He's the brains of the two and the strongest man on the island. Been to our dry dock many times," Betty informed us. Paco nodded in agreement.

"Don't worry, my friends. Zep has been away for several weeks to the mainland. By the time he returns, you'll be long gone," Jose said to comfort us. Tobi looked worried and only somewhat comforted.

After another round of beers, Tobi touched my hand. I nodded my accord. "We appreciate everything everyone has done for us, but we wanted to see some of Oak Ridge tomorrow, so we'd better call it a day," I told them.

"You'll always be welcome here," Jose told us, with Maria and the Sylvesters agreeing.

"I'll be glad to get out of this place," Tobi said when we were aboard Magic.

"I can understand that," I said. "We'll move on in the morning."

We spent the remainder of the evening reviewing our cruising guide to the Bay Islands. It described Oak Ridge as a quiet piscatorial settlement and the end of the island bus line, and the road itself ended there. We thought this might be a nice place to spend a few days and were hoping for an end to the type of excitement we had experienced in French Harbor. It was only a four-hour trip, but I wanted to check the charts for the next day's excursion. By the time I called it a night, Tobi and the canines were fast asleep.

#

"Nate, what are you doing here?" The heavily muscled Zep peered through the crack in the door. Opening the door wide, he greeted the uncle of his friend.

Nate took Zep's hand. Though Nate was a lot taller than Zep, who was of average height, Zep's strength was legendary throughout the Bay islands. But it wasn't for being crazy and dangerous. Still, Carlos was his sister's pet, and he needed Zep.

CHAPTER 4

Coco woke me bright and early. Tobi was already making coffee.

"Hi, Honey," she said cheerfully as I made my way to the table. Setting a cup of hot coffee in front of me, she added, "You'd better hurry and wake up. Jose and Maria said they were going to see us off."

It was only a short run to Oak Ridge, but with only two people aboard Magic, I spent the next hour checking that everything was battened down and the launch was secure on the davits. High winds, rough water, a line squall, or countless other problems could make two people pretty busy on a yacht the size of Magic. But with the proper preparation and everything in place, we could usually handle whatever came up.

When the Romeos showed at eight-thirty, I promised that we would return next year if our wandering schedule permitted. Soon, we were clear of the channel and headed east. With the wind at fifteen knots going north by east, we raised Magic's genoa, mizzen, and main sails and enjoyed the trip up the southern coast of Roatan Island. Finding the coast littered with the various-sized wrecks from yachts to freighters, we were reminded that the weather was not always as nice as we were now having. The warning was well taken, we decided, as we viewed the rocky coast. The mountainous ridges were covered with thick green vegetation and armies of large trees. Since there were few inhabitants outside the settlements, they never noticed a living soul on their run up the coast.

Around noon, Tobi pointed to a white church standing on a hill at the western end of the Oak Ridge settlement. Over the port bow, we watched the spray form waves breaking over the rocks that stood guard over Oak Ridge Harbor. The cut between them was marked with a tall rotating light standing high on the rocks, east of the cut.

"Tobi, that rotating light looks like an old gas pump. The ones they used to pump by hand. Doesn't it?"

"What makes you think I'm old enough to remember that?"

Deciding to keep my mouth shut, I lined up on the cut. Then Tobi took over the wheel while I lowered the sails and began getting them ferruled and reefed. She started the diesel engine and maneuvered until I retook the control. The diesel engine, allowing for better control and maneuverability in close quarters, helped greatly, especially since the cut was narrow and the harbor fairly small.

"Look, Honey. The water's crystal clear. You can see the slab rock twenty feet down on the bottom." To the inexperienced eye, it appeared to be only a foot, but Tobi was a very experienced diver, having instructed on many occasions during our years in Florida.

Just inside the harbor to the east, a handsome building constructed of cyprus with a cedar-shingled roof stood on pilings surrounded by water with a dock in front and on both ends. A large sign proclaimed that the location was the Oak Ridge Discotheque.

"We won't have to worry about drunk-driving tickets on the way home from there," Tobi said.

I smiled. "Yeah, we can boogie down without a care." I spotted a small cove toward the back of the bay and headed for it. "We'll stay out about two hundred yards from shore."

Tobi nodded in agreement. I turned the wheel over to her command and headed forward to prepare the anchor. I was eager for a few days of rest and some leisure reading. I might even challenge Magic's scrabble champion to a rematch. After hustling to get the hook down, we settled down on the aft deck under the sun awning.

"Finally, peace and quiet," I said.

"Not for long," Tobi replied, indicating a small aluminum launch that appeared to be heading their way.

We watched the craft on its approach until it came alongside Magic. It's one occupant, sporting a long gray beard with long hair to match, sat smoking an ugly crooked pipe.

"May I come aboard?"

"Sure," I said, helping him string his launch off the stern.

As the man's feet touched the deck, he nodded hello to me.

"Afternoon, folks. Go by Randy Lewis, most of the time."

I introduced Tobi and myself.

"Are you folks from the U.S.?"

"Well, we live in Guatemala now, after we left Florida several years ago," I answered.

"Aye. Lived in Florida myself before I came to the Bay Islands many years ago. Do all the electrical fixin' around here. When I ain't working the plant there," he said, indicating the fish processing plant that lay across the harbor. "This is a really nice sailer you have here," he said approvingly.

"Thank you," Tobi said.

"That's my beauty there," Randy said, pointing to an odd-looking boat that sat anchored in the direction of the plant. "I call her the 'Ark'. I guess you can see why."

We had to agree. It did resemble something Noah might have built. Randy began filling us in on what was happening in Oak Ridge. According to our friendly source, the disco we had passed coming in was only open on weekends, but the Happy Landing would be a pleasant place to spend an evening. With three pool tables and a jukebox, the food was worthy of investigation.

"There are mostly locals," Randy said, indicating the direction of the Happy Landing a half-mile up one of the canals. He cast his gaze slowly around Magic's deck. "We don't see too many fancy yachts up this far."

Everything was either near the harbor or up one of the many canals. Since there was only one road and few vehicles, all the homes and businesses were on the water and traveling was usually by boat.

"Where are the best diving areas?" Tobi asked.

"You people come to dive?" Randy asked with surprise.

"Sure, we've got our own air compressor to fill our tank," I said.

I explained that Tobi had an instructor's certificate from Florida and that I'd been through UDT School during a stint in the U.S. Navy.

"Sounds like you're both qualified scuba divers," Randy agreed. "But I can't really recommend anything close by. Most people go to a diving resort around at Antony's Cay on the other side of the island. Plenty of good diving but dad burned expensive if you take one of those diving tours."

We both were silent, then Tobi answered, "We'd rather be off to ourselves."

"Yeah, we like to poke around on our own," I agreed.

Randy scratched his beard. "There's the Hog Cays. Just a few fishermen. Spear fishing's great. Further east, there are some old wrecks you might find interesting."

"What about Old Port Royal Bay?" Tobi asked, in a tone that was carefully casual.

Randy looked uneasy. "It's guarded by Fowler Reef. I wouldn't go there."

"It seems like a well-known pirate stronghold would be a great place to dive," I argued.

"Well . . . some of the locals have found a few gold coins, but nobody goes there anymore."

"Sure sounds good to me," I said. "There should be all kinds of artifacts around there."

Randy nodded in agreement. "But when the sea gets rough, Fowler Reef is treacherous. I hear that there's a bunch of caves and undercuts on the outside face of the reef. They say it creates some crazy currents. After you get down thirty feet or so."

"It sounds dangerous," Tobi agreed.

"Seven locals have disappeared diving the reef. They call it the old Widow Maker."

"They ever find any of them?" I asked.

"No. And . . ." Randy hesitated. "They say it's haunted." He waited for the effect of his statement.

Tobi and I looked at each other questioningly. "By the seven locals?" she asked.

"No, by all the prisoners murdered by the pirates," he answered matter-of-factual.

"Well, we don't believe in ghosts much," I said.

"I do know that an American and his wife had some problems there."

Tobi looked concerned. "What kind of problems?" she asked.

Randy explained how the couple had sailed into Old Port Royal Bay in a fancy yacht like ours and had fallen in love with the spot. After buying land on the northern and eastern shore of the bay, they had begun building a marina and yacht club with the idea of luring cruising yachts from the Bahamas. Randy had introduced himself to them about six years ago in the same manner as today at about the same spot. Therefore, he was acquainted enough to say hello on occasions. They were hard working and industrious and had begun to make progress with the dock and a large building, which was to become the bar and clubhouse.

"Still standing today. Rundown, but still standing," he added, puffing on his pipe and staring into space.

"Well, what happened?" Tobi demanded.

"No one knows for sure, but . . . this is how the old timers tell it. I can vouch for that."

We listened intently as Randy spun the tale.

#

Hurricane-type winds were bending the trees like they were made of rubber. The bay rocked in frustration, causing the couple alarm. Fortunately, their seventy-foot yacht was moored securely to the dock for the moment. Dave Menton leaned over the stalled engine that generated electricity from the small power house at the end of the dock. Drenched by the rain-filled winds, he tried to start the engine once more, a strain even for strong arms. Hearing a noise behind him, he turned. "Hon—" Before he could finish, his head fell to the floor and rolled several feet. The blue eyes stared in surprise.

A large black man stood, dripping wet from the rain, hunched and alert, surveying the grisly scene that he had just created. His wild eyes continued to move swiftly about as he wiped blood from the machete.

He wiped the blood on his pants. As his bare feet strolled through the red flood spurting from the headless corpse, his only thoughts were on the white woman with the blond hair. The one who had tormented him while he worked. Wearing those skimpy bathing suits, she had tormented him with her body for the last time. He made his way down the dock towards the moored yacht. The winds, attempting to push him back, could not stop him.

The captain's wife, Nancy, sick from the boat's movement, tried to gather a few items to take ashore while they waited out the storm. Expecting the sound of approaching steps to be Dave returning from the power house, she was surprised when rough black hands grabbed her from behind.

Pulling her down by the hair, the intruder stared at her bare breasts, exposed by the tear in her blouse. Forcing her mouth to his unbuttoned trousers, he screamed in pain when she bit down as hard as she could. Falling back, he grabbed his injured friend with both hands. Through the pain, he could see her frantically searching through a drawer. He picked up his machete from where he had dropped it and slung it as a shot rang out. The blade struck her at an odd angle, injuring her shoulder. As he watched her, a hole bloomed in the middle of his forehead. His friend was no longer in pain.

Nancy held a shirt to the wound until the bleeding stopped. After several anxious attempts to radio for help, she went searching for her husband. The wind pushed her from the dock towards the shore as it continued to wreak havoc throughout the night.

The next day, the sky was bright and the bay showed no signs of the previous night's horrors. A power boat belonging to one of their new friends from the area motored up to the dock. They had become acquainted after beginning the work on the proposed marina. Having received a report of the frantic radio calls, the new arrival had hurried to his friend's aid.

Seeing bloody footprints going on and off the yacht, his whole body tensed and he began looking anxiously around for any signs of danger to his new friends. After finding the body of the intruder, mired in blood, he went looking for Nancy. To his shock, he saw the woman sitting on the rough planking of the new dock. She was rocking back and forth, staring at what only she could see. With the severed head of her late husband lying in her lap, she stroked the unanticipated trophy gently, her hands moving very slowly.

#

"God, that's a gruesome story," Tobi said shaking her head.

"What happened to her?"

"Well, they patched her up in La Ceiba, Honduras, but she wouldn't speak to anybody or eat. Finally, the U.S. embassy found a relative who came and got her. Had some charter captain take the yacht back to the States."

"I can see why nobody goes there anymore," I remarked.

"Probably the most private place around the Bay Islands."

"Randy, you don't really put any stock in those haunted stories, do you?" Tobi asked.

"Course not. But on the other hand, lots of people who used to dive off the Widow Maker ain't round no more," he answered.

"Well, the story about the American couple was tragic, but I'm still interested in the coins and stuff the locals used to bring up off Fowler Reef. You know where they came from?" I asked. I ignored Tobi's warning glare.

"Lots of stories going round," he said, stuffing fresh tobacco from a small leather pouch into his crooked pipe.

"Probably from the pirate era, don't you think?" Tobi asked.

"Well," he began, as he lit a match to his pipe and began puffing on it. "You know how people like to talk. Most of the locals claim to be descended from the pirates that considered Roatan their property." He described how treasure ships, loaded to the gunnels with gold, silver, and every sort of jewel-encrusted items you could imagine, would leave Panama bound for Spain. Coming close to the islands of Guanaja or Roatan, they would run north along the east coast of Nicaragua. Pirates based in Old Port Royal, at the east end of Roatan, would lie in wait.

Captured ships, if they remained afloat, were brought back to the pirates' stronghold. The crews and passengers of the captured ships were then held for ransom, sold as slaves, or used for sport—whatever took the fancy of their captors. Legend had it that Old Port Royal had been the final resting place for possibly hundreds of unlucky souls who had fallen prey to the pirates of Port Royal.'

"Do you suppose any of those coins are still around?" I asked.

Tobi stood up rather abruptly, looking annoyed. "Can I get anyone a drink? Coffee or whatever?" She hoped to change the subject or silence her talkative spouse. They both declined her offer, but she had slowed them down.

"Might be. Don't know for sure, but I could ask a few of the locals."

"I'd sure like to look at what's been found around here."

"Well, I'll see if I can come up with something. Are you interested in buying any?"

"If it's possible, but I'd rather like to try and date one."

"Do you have some expertise on the subject?" Randy inquired.

"Like I said, diving is a love of my wife and I. We've dived on several wrecks around the Florida Keys and the Bahamas. We've even tried the Silver Banks off the Dominican Republic and Cape Haitian, where the Santa Maria sunk."

"Sounds like you two have done your share of diving. Ever find anything . . . you know, valuable?"

"Nothing valuable, but we love looking," Tobi answered.

"You know, they have a lot of records on ships that never made port after leaving Panama over in Puerto Cortes on the mainland. I tried looking them over myself once, but I can't make heads or tails of Spanish."

"They also have a good archives library at the Saint Carlo's University in Guatemala," Tobi informed him. She had spent hours poring over dozens of volumes that covered the period from 1620 to 1750. She had even found information on several ships that could have disappeared around Roatan or Guanaja.

"She spent enough time there," I agreed. "There are quite a few ships suspected of sinking in the area of the Bay Islands. That's mainly why we want to spend some time here. Who knows? We might even get lucky."

"That's what dreams are made of," Randy said. "Just let me know if you need any help. I'll ask around about any old coins and let you know."

"We'd appreciate it," Tobi said.

"You can catch me anytime there on the Ark or give me a call on the radio. I monitor channel 18, as most folks around here do."

We promised, if we decided to go out later that evening, to buy Randy a drink at the Happy Landing. We watched as Randy's launch retreated toward the seafood factory.

"Wow, the time really flew," I said, looking at my watch.

"He was a talker," she agreed. "And you talked a little more than you needed to."

I held up a half-full glass. "It was the liquor talking."

"I know. I just think we need to be careful about what we say. We don't know who we can trust around here."

As we relaxed on the aft deck, the day came to a close. The horizon, becoming a spectacular orange ball, could only be appreciated by someone who had spent time anchored in the Caribbean. Feeling blessed, I caressed my wife's neck as we watched the sunset.

"Jim, what do you think of Randy's story of Old Port Royal?"

I knew her thoughts. She had spent a lot of time researching that particular spot. We had already decided to concentrate our diving efforts there. "Well, it's something to think about. I'm not too worried about ghosts. But I am very curious about the currents and undertows around Fowler Reef. Do you remember the caves off Andros Island near the tongue of the ocean?"

"I remember what happened to that Navy diver from the research station at Morgan's Bluff. Hadn't they been trying to set a new underwater scuba record?"

"They had previously, but at this time they were exploring an underwater cave in the cliff side," I said.

"Right. The diver had taken his tank and diving gear off at the three-hundred foot level."

"It's believed that the incident was caused by nitrogen narcosis."

"That's nasty stuff."

"It is. With an excess of nitrogen, the diver has a feeling of well-being and false belief that they can do impossible things such as taking a breath under water."

"What a horrible way to die. They found some of his equipment, didn't they?"

I shook my head sadly. "Yes, but not the body. I remember that incident. I also remember there was a theory that those caves were tied to the Blue Holes." The famous Blue Holes were numerous in the Bahamas. Most of the undertow and underwater currents in the area were caused by the tides and water that was said to move through the caves, believed to link to tunnels formed by ocean currents over millions of years.

"I remember when we were diving that Blue Hole near Delectable Bay about the same time. God, that's been twenty years. What made you remember that?" Tobi asked.

"Just wondering if that might be why so many divers disappeared off Fowler Reef. It's a possibility. If the caves of Andros Island are tied to the Blue Holes of the Bahama Banks, why couldn't the underwater caves here be also?"

"So what would that mean? For a diver?"

"Think about all the pressure, suction, and forces created when the ocean tide moves. This could have an effect in caves and undersea tunnels hundreds of miles away—and on the persons and objects in them."

"It's an interesting theory."

"Could you imagine the suction created in the mouth of an underwater cave down here off Roatan when the tide was running off the Bank?"

"Wow, I can see what you mean. You wouldn't have a chance if you were caught in an undertow of that force. Maybe we should scratch Port Royal. Damn, I was really looking forward to spending some time there," she said.

"Well, honey, why don't we wait to make any decision until I have a chance to do some figuring on the tides here and in the Bahamas."

We had a light supper aboard Magic and were enjoying the solitude so much that we decided to pass up drinks at the Happy Landing. We would wait until the next day before meeting new friends and seeking fun and excitement.

At mealtime, we continued our talk of the pending adventure. "I want both of us to be very up to date on tidal information," I said. "I want both of us to play 'what if' with our every move. Tobi, you are a very bright lady and I depend on you more than you know. So don't forget to pull me up if I get careless, okay?"

CHAPTER 5

Tobi and I arose early and watched the sun make its way over the rugged hills of Roatan. The reflections off the bay water and stainless steel rigging of the yacht were enough to dissipate the recent trials and disappointments of our lives. Holding my wife close, I enjoyed the beauty and peace of the island.

"Jim, why don't we go ashore and see if the market has any fresh vegetables?"

"Good idea. I wouldn't mind doing some sightseeing. Why don't you get organized below while I let the whaler off the stern davits and check the gas and motor?"

The Boston Whaler was fourteen foot and was powered with a twenty-five horse-powered Evinrude. We depended on the whaler to get us safely to shore and back. Especially since we spent most of our cruising time at anchor rather than moored to a dock. While this gave us more privacy, we had to keep a generator for power and a good supply of water aboard to lessen our needs from shore.

I had the whaler in the water and ready to go by the time Tobi strolled on deck announcing she was ready. She looked stunning with a white pair of shorts and black T-shirt displaying an anchor and the name "Magic" in gold. I checked out her legs and moved my eyes up to her pretty face.

"You know you might get me mugged in town. I'll have to fight every guy around to keep 'em away from you."

"Oh, stop it. You're buttering me up for some reason. Did you forget my birthday?" she asked with a smile.

"I don't think so. When is it?" I replied, ducking a playful swing in my direction.

I headed the whaler across the bay to the sea food factory pier. "This looks as good a place as any. The market's supposed to be a kilometer that way." I pointed past the factory towards the settlement. We began our walk towards the open market where the people still use barter as their main order of business. Anyone with something to sell would be there. From early morning to mid-day, the village market was the busiest place for miles around. I just hoped our whaler would still be tied to the end of the pier when we returned.

"Do you think that man on the dock will watch our boat like he promised?" Tobi asked. She held firmly to my hand.

"I don't know. The eager way he agreed, he might plan on selling it. But I think it'll be all right," I added. As we walked on the dirt lane that crossed behind the factory, we began passing several small one-room shacks made of cane poles and mud. We noticed an old woman standing at the entrance of one while she moved the dirt around with a thatched broom.

Tobi stopped in the path and asked the woman, "Is this the road to the market?"

The old woman looked at us suspiciously. "Ain't but one road. Ain't but one market." I started to duck as the old lady swung her broom in the direction of the market. "So, you just go on up there, you run right into it," she said, waving her broom in the air.

We thanked her, and, ducking the possessed broom, we went up the lane hand in hand like a couple on their first date. Before long, we spied the market place, a cluster of cane stalls measuring eight feet across the front and eight feet deep. There were close to fifty of them, filled with various products of the island. We had our choice of chickens or ducks, coconut bread, sweet cakes, and masa, or tortilla dough, for the stomach. The dry goods consisted of cloth, woven baskets, and beads and jewelry made from shells. For the seafood enthusiast, there was enough fresh fish, dried fish, shrimp, and lobster to supply several restaurants.

We meandered our way through, looking at everything, enjoying the sight of the brightly-dressed people. Most of the stall operators were black women dressed gaily in every color of the rainbow. Some wore brightly-colored turbans wound around their heads, but they all wore scads of native jewelry. Tobi and I were enjoying the friendly atmosphere and headed towards the area with fresh vegetables and new-cut flowers ahead on our right. A young teenaged local attached himself to us.

"Hey, Captain. You and the beautiful lady off the black boat in the harbor?" he asked in English.

"Yes, why?" I answered.

"You need a guide. I am the best."

"No thank you. We're doing fine."

"You need someone to show you best places. I can get best prices in the market, carry your bags, clean your boat, and I can protect you."

"Protect us from what?" I inquired.

"Many pirates around here," the youngster said matter-of-factly.

"I think we'll be fine. Thank you anyway."

The boy lagged behind us as we made their way to a vegetable stand where Tobi began haggling over prices. I stood back and enjoyed the exchange. Finally, after she had purchased several small tomatoes, onions, peppers, and carrots, she decided we'd had enough marketing for the day.

We began retracing our steps towards our floating home-away-from-home. The settlement didn't have much to offer except for small cluttered shacks facing the bay or one of the canals with their backs to the dirt lane. As we strolled through what passed for a town, the young black man caught up with us.

"Hey, Captain."

"Yes." I said as we continued to walk.

"Would you maybe like to buy some old silver pieces of eight?"

We stopped and looked at him. "You have some silver pieces of eight?" I asked.

The boy nodded. "Not with me, but I could go get them."

I looked at Tobi, who shrugged. "I could take a look, but I don't know if I'm interested or not."

"I'll go get them. It will take me awhile, but I could bring them to your boat this afternoon."

Tobi nodded her agreement to me, and I replied, "Okay, that'll be fine. We'll see you later and take a look at your pieces of eight."

The youngster smiled and shook his head in agreement, then rushed up a small trail that led into the hills. Do you think it'd be wise to let him come aboard Magic?" Tobi asked.

"It'll be all right. He's harmless."

As we came to the seafood factory, a large following of naked black children had gathered to beg for money, so we decided we'd seen enough of Oak Ridge. It was much more appealing from the boat, the bay and distance adding quietness and beauty. We decided it was not very quiet up close. When we arrived at the whaler, our watchman was on duty and assured us that he had watched it well. I handed him five *lempiras,* or about two dollars, and thanked him. We loaded our vegetables aboard the launch and started across the bay towards Magic.

#

The black man leaning against the factory building sneered as he watched the whaler head for Magic. They hadn't recognized him out of his uniform. Nate knew that Carlos would be pleased to know his friends were nearby

The ex-security guard of their earlier meeting had been told by Carlos to keep an eye on the Americans from the black yacht and to keep him informed of their travels in the Bay Islands and their interests. If he could find out what they liked and what they were interested in, he could find a way to turn a profit at their expense. After all, he lived by his wits and the mistakes and vices of the unsuspecting. It was the only life he had ever known. This kind of happy couple with their ducks in a row were his kind of prey.

#

After helping Tobi aboard, I strung the launch off the stern. Tobi opened the screen door, allowing Coco and Peanut out on deck. They yapped their appreciation, happy to be free. After settling down on the aft deck, Tobi asked, "What do you think of the man with the pieces of eight?"

"I don't really know. He puts me in mind of a hustler, but we'll have to wait and see."

We were just finished cleaning up after lunch when I spotted a cayuco heading in our direction. We watched it approach for nearly ten minutes before we recognized their silver salesman. He came alongside and greeted us. We answered in unison and the youth tossed up the thin nylon line secured to the cayuco from a hole cut in the wood forming the bow. I caught it and invited him aboard. As he climbed over the rail, I strung the dugout off the stern alongside the whaler. All three of us sat at the table in the cockpit and the teenager pulled a dirty red bandanna from his shirt pocket.

"These pieces are very old, Captain," he said. He unwrapped the bandanna. "Some divers brought them up from down around Hog Cay. Worth lots of money in

United States. Here on Roatan, we don't have chance for fair price. We take what we can get." Finished with his speech, he proffered the pieces of metal to me. Tobi stood beside the table and peered over his shoulder.

"I make you a special price."

We stared at the dull-looking square pieces of metal for several minutes, before I returned them to the salesman.

"I believe we'll pass on these."

The teenager looked rejected. "How come, Captain? I make you real good deal."

"I'm sure you would, but we really don't have any extra cash with us to purchase them. So, no thank you."

"Maybe you trade."

"No. I'm not interested at this time. Thank you for your trouble, but we're expecting a call from home, and you'll have to excuse us."

"Okay. Maybe I find something else," he said, re-wrapping his coins to leave. I untied the line securing the cayuco to the stern and pulled it alongside for our departing visitor.

"So long, Captain, Missus. See you again," he said, climbing down to his boat.

"Sure," I said. I waved goodbye to the dugout heading for Oak Ridge.

We stepped inside the pilot house and took a seat at the dinette.

"The coins weren't very good, were they?" Tobi asked.

"Horrible. Looked like Babbitt with a little silver and zinc thrown in. About the worst I've ever seen," I exclaimed. I had seen hundreds of phony pieces of eight in my travels through the islands and the Florida Keys. Some were cleverly done, but not these. "I didn't feel like hurting his pride or creating hard feelings, so I thought my approach was the best way."

"I know, but I sure wanted to say something. I wanted you to decide how to handle him, so I held my tongue."

After a quick swim, we decided to take a short nap before going ashore for dinner, and then planned to pay the Happy Landing a visit. About seven o'clock, we climbed into the whaler for our trip ashore. Decked out in shorts, Magic T-shirts, and top-siders, we motored across the bay into the main canal that ran through Oak Ridge.

There was a narrow strip of land about a hundred yards wide that ran south of Roatan for several miles and formed the canal. The waterway was about thirty yards wide at the entrance. Wharf's, mostly on the northern mainland, lined the canal. Docks on the southern strip were mostly for private houses, small restaurants, and bars, like the Happy Landing, which lay dead ahead. "Let's go on up farther and see if a restaurant catches my eye," Tobi suggested.

Leaving all restaurant decisions to Tobi, I continued west along the canal for another mile until she tapped my hand.

"I like the looks of that place," she said, pointing to an establishment on the right.

I agreed, angling toward the sturdy dock that fronted it. Five steps, complete with one-inch lines running through posts on each side, led up to the open-air establishment that proclaimed itself to be Mother Brown's Restaurant on a gaudy orange hand-painted signboard. The raised floor of the restaurant appeared to be unpainted cypress that matched the rest of the structure. Though unpainted, the place was very neat in appearance with just the right touch of island atmosphere. The dining area, bordered with attractive rails, consisted of small wooden tables for four with red and white checkered table coverings. Tying the launch securely to the dock, we climbed onto the deck. A very overweight, black woman standing at the rail above greeted us with the widest and brightest smile.

"You all come on up here and have the best food on the island or I ain't Mother Brown, and I sure is."

"Good evening," we chorused, climbing the stairs to her level.

Exchanging pleasantries, she inquired if we were off the yacht, Magic. After our confirmation, she guided us to a table near the rail with a beautiful view of the canal, where there were areas void of buildings and you could see the ocean itself. We agreed with her suggestion of red snapper and decided to have a beer while we waited. After another beer with the delicious red snapper, Tobi bragged, "You got to admit it; I always spot the best food around."

"You're my favorite guide," I assured her. "No matter where we happen to be, you find just the right place."

As we relaxed and made small talk, we spotted Randy Lewis in his beat-up aluminum launch nosing into the pier alongside the whaler. We greeted him as he was getting out of his launch.

"I see you managed to find the best food on the island."

"Yeah, Tobi's the expert restaurant picker. Are you just coming to dinner?" I asked Randy.

"Oh, no. I just noticed your launch wasn't trailing Magic, so I decided to cruise down the canal till I spotted you."

"Any special reason?" I asked.

"Thought I'd invite you over to the Happy Landing for a beer and some more stimulating conversation."

"Sure, I'm open for anything."

I paid the tab and we descended the steps where Randy was waiting with the launches. We followed him to the dock facing the Happy Landing and went inside.

The main attraction of the large, one-room establishment was the three pool tables in the center area of the room. A U-shaped bar with wooden stools stood against the center rear wall with several wooden tables, complete with matching chairs to the left end of the room. The right end was reserved for dancing. The wooden floor cried for varnish as did everything else; all was unpainted and bare of decoration.

Several people were scattered around the room. After we entered, a nice-looking Latin man in his mid-forties greeted Randy warmly, then greeted Tobi and me. He introduced himself as Augusto, the owner, and insisted that we have their first drink on him. We obliged him, and, seating ourselves, began soaking up the relaxed atmosphere. Being more of a family tavern than a bar, the patrons were either fishermen or local business operators.

The locals began drifting over, one or two at a time, until we had several tables together and a loud friendly drinking party in progress. One of the fellows Augusto introduced was Brut Sanders who owned the ice plant, general store, and several lobster boats, all located at the western canal entrance. We had noticed the prosperous-looking business situated on the right bank as we left the Bay and moved into the canal. Brut, a large, red-faced man of nearly sixty years appeared to have enjoyed his life to the fullest and soaked up more than his share of whiskey in the process. Tobi couldn't help but notice all the gold jewelry that Burt was wearing. Especially a very old, rough-cut gold coin that hung from a heavy gold chain around his neck set in a coil of wire rope.

"I really like your gold coin. Where did you get it?" she asked.

"Bought the thing from one of the local lads who used to dive for lobster up around Fowler Reef. Had the setting made up special over in La Ceiba."

"It looks really old," she replied.

"Jeweler said it was stamped in Lima, Peru, in 1620. Said it was pretty valuable, even though I'd never sell it."

"Do you think the fellow you bought it from has any more?" I asked.

"Well, he could have, but it'd be kinda late to ask him."

"Where could I reach him?"

"Last time anyone saw him, he was diving for lobster off Fowler Reef. Just never came up again." Tobi gave me a worried look.

"Wonder if there are any more coins to be found," I said absently.

"Be careful . . .," Burt advised. "Or the Widow Maker will get you too."

I was disappointed that I wouldn't be able to question the diver, but the possibility that the coin came from the ocean around Roatan excited me. We continued to enjoy the conversation with the islanders until Tobi decided that Augusto, who had been drinking steadily, was showing more interest in her than she was in the mood for. So we took our leave while Randy, who was staying on, promised to drop by our boat the next day.

"Glad we left when we did. I thought I was going to have to hurt Augusto's feelings," Tobi said as she seated herself in the whaler.

"I noticed. He looked like he fell in love with the wrong girl."

"Glad you noticed. I thought you were so engrossed in conversation that you had forgotten me."

"Not a chance, Kid," I said, putting my hand on her knee. "The conversation doesn't get that interesting."

"You'd better say that," she warned.

As I climbed aboard Magic, instead of raising the whaler on the davits, I strung the launch to one of the stern cleats.

"Look at all the stars," Tobi said. Seems as if you can almost reach out and touch one."

"Just like the phone company."

"Cute, but why do they seem so much closer on the water than from land?"

"Maybe because on land there's more light to take away from them. On the water they'd seem brighter, therefore closer."

"You're so clever. You're probably right," she said stifling a yawn.

"You're making me tired," I said playfully.

"Let's turn in so we can do some exploring up the canals tomorrow."

I agreed and followed her below.

#

As Nate sat in his launch wondering how he had been conned into waiting for Zep and Carlos, he spied the whaler pulling alongside Magic. Strange, the American wasn't raising it on the davits, but leaving it tied to the stern. As he watched, he decided to surprise his cohorts.

Zep and the young girls watched the jailer's wife leave the jail. Built of cinder block, the building appeared to have been built a long time ago. Since it was doubtful that Carlos would remain on the honor system, the jailer had been ordered to sleep over until Carlos was transferred to the mainland.

"About time that bitch left." Zep cursed. It had been dark for an hour. "Do you know what to do?" he asked the pretty olive complected sixteen-year-old.

"I'm not going to fuck that fat slob," she exclaimed.

"Look, I told you, Just get him away from there. How hard can that be?" Zep sounded pissed.

Nayrita recognized the beginnings of a foul mood. She snuggled close to him.

"You're the only man for me."

"What are you saying," he sneered. "Carlos was screwing you when I met you."

"I'm not a whore," she screamed, pushing away from him.

"Hey," he said pulling her close to keep her quiet. "You're the one I think of always," he said. He stroked her face softly. Wiping a tear from the corner of her eye, he continued, "I have to get the jailer away. You don't want me to have to hurt your daddy's best friend to get Carlos out, do you?"

"No, then Daddy would never let me see you."

"Just keep him away from here for thirty minutes."

Zep watched her walk towards the jail, her hips swaying seductively. The puta's got a body on her, he thought. She stopped before opening the door and looked his way. Blowing him a kiss, she swung the door open and walked in.

"Nayrita, what're you doin' here?" Juan asked. He sat up on the cot where he had been lying. He eyed her short skirt and the full bosom scarcely concealed by her peasant blouse unbuttoned at the top. His mouth dried as always when his friend's daughter was around.

"Have you seen my daddy?" she asked licking her upper lip.

"No, is there something wrong?" he asked as he stood awkwardly.

She looked at the five foot six, two hundred-eighty pound guard and started to lose her nerve. Then she smiled, her mind working quickly.

"I was walking home when I saw some men lurking along the canal. I was afraid. Could you walk me home?"

Juan looked through the old-fashioned bars right out of the old west at his sleeping prisoner. "I guess I could," he said, trying to hide the excitement in his voice.

Zep watched the deputy lock the door behind him as the two started walking towards Nayrita's home. Holding on to the guard's arm, she appeared to have everything under control. Zep sneered. They made a good couple.

He ran across the clearing to the back of the jail. During his last visit, he had noticed that the bars in the window were close to falling out on their own.

"Carlos," he whispered through the window. He heard a noise below, then a face appeared.

"Zep! Thank God you're here."

"You're lucky I showed up to save your sorry ass."

Carlos hung his head. "Yeah, I know. I shouldn't have been working while you were gone." He stared in surprise as Zep's bulging biceps tore a bar out of the window. "Damn!" the next bar was a little more difficult, but using the freed bar as a lever, Zep soon worked it free. Carlos's slim body was soon able to squeeze through the opening left by the missing two bars.

"You're not going to believe this," Carlos said.

"What?"

"I think Nayrita has the hots for Juan."

Zep roared with laughter as they walked away. Ten minutes later, a depressed Juan unlocked the jail door. His lips had been pressed to one of her firm breasts with her hand stroking his cock, when suddenly she had left him lying in the bushes where they had stopped. By the time he had pulled his pants up, she was long gone. Now, looking at the vacant cell, his mouth hung open.

Nate was waiting in the shadows of the seafood factory when Zep and Carlos appeared on the dock. Jumping into view, he startled them. Zep, pissed off at being startled, started to punch Nate in the face.

"Why in the hell did you do that?" Zep asked.

Nate replied, "Come on, I've got something to show you."

Zep, anxious to get away, motioned for Carlos to follow him into Nate's launch. "What do ya have to show me?" Zep asked as Nate started toward the ice plant.

Nate said, "I stashed it among the lobster boats."

Carlos recognized the Boston Whaler as they pulled alongside. "Where is that American bastard?" he said. "I want to kill him."

"We don't have time for that," Zep growled. He climbed into the whaler and started to examine the twenty-five horsepower Evinrude. "This is really nice. You can kill him later, but now we have to get busy."

They removed supplies from Burt's general store and stored them in Zep's new launch. "Meet us at the shack in three days with more supplies. Also, I need more shells for my pistol," Zep said.

Nate agreed to bring their supplies and them head toward the eastern canal. He was grateful that Zep had refused to carry through with his intent to kill the American. He really didn't want to be part of that. It was bad enough to be involved in Carlos's escape.

Carlos gritted his teeth in hatred as he spotted Magic anchored across the bay. He would meet the American again.

CHAPTER 6

Up early, I could see the tell-tale signs of a light tropical rain having fallen during the night. Though just a touch of hazy mist remained over the water, the sky was clear and the morning promised beautiful new adventures. Standing in the stern cockpit, I admired the view offered by the surrounding bay.

But as I listened to the rattling sounds of Tobi preparing breakfast, something began nagging at the back of my mind. Staring past the stern of the yacht, I was aware that something was different. Finally I snapped to attention. The Boston Whaler wasn't strung on its line behind Magic where it should have been. Stepping up to the deck, I looked at the cleat where the line from the launch was still made fast. I bent over and pulled the line to me. About ten feet of line was dangling loose in the water. I could see that the line had been cut clean. The whaler was gone! My first reaction was surprise, then I realized that someone had swum or rowed out to Magic during the night. Another prowler! This violation of privacy, added to our experiences at French Harbor, began to really steam me and worry me at the same time. What next, I wondered?

I was still trying to keep from boiling over when Tobi called from below in her especially cheerful voice, bubbling with friendliness and goodwill, that breakfast was ready. Wanting to scream, who the fuck cares, I began calming down at the sound of her voice. I considered how I should tell her that we had been violated again and the whaler was gone. I knew how fond she was of our attractive satellite to Magic, and we both knew that it would be impossible to replace it here in the Bay Islands. Deciding to face it, I turned and went below for breakfast. As we sat at the dinette, Tobi was in such a good mood and so primed for adventure that I hated to deflate her spirits with bad news.

"You're being so quiet. You don't have a hangover from too much beer do you?"

"No, but someone cut the line and took the whaler." There! It was out.

She was quiet for a moment, but when the news began to soak in, she looked as though she was going to cry. "I can't believe it. Why would anyone do that? Where could they go with it? Everyone would know it was stolen."

"Well, Honey, you know most of the locals are descended from pirates. I guess it's probably in their blood."

"That's great. What are we going to do now? We can't buy one around here."

"We can't replace it here for sure, but we still have the Avon inflatable, and I can get out that five horse-powered Yamaha that's stored in the dive locker."

She began to calm herself, realizing that at least we had the Avon.

I continued. "I'll break it out and pump it up with the foot pump. At least I can go ashore and report it."

"Jim, I want out of these damn islands. There's more pirates running around today than three hundred years ago."

"I agree. It seems like problems everywhere we stop."

"It's just not worth the hassle," she said. "I'm starting to wonder what's next."

I thought for a moment. "Let me break out the Avon and take a run over to shore and see what I can find out. Then we'll see. The Bay Islands are beginning to sour for me also. Just don't let this upset you too much. We'll work something out."

I went on deck and opened the large white locker bolted to the fore deck that had served as a hiding place for our prowler only three days earlier. I began setting diving tanks, spare mooring lines, dive weights, and other equipment on the deck until I came to two canvas-covered bundles at the bottom that contained a 12 foot Avon rubber inflatable and the five horse-powered Yamaha outboard that I kept for emergencies. I rummaged around until I found the foot pump to save myself several hours of blowing air into the Avon. I laid the deflated launch flat out on the deck and hooked up the hose that goes to the accordion-looking device. As I began the foot-action that pumps the air, mumbling and cussing to myself the entire time, I spotted Randy in his beat-up aluminum launch headed our way. I continued the foot action until Randy was almost alongside, then I gave my foot a rest while I went aft to take Randy's line.

"Where's your whaler?" Randy asked as he climbed aboard.

"Wish I knew. Some bastard cut the line and borrowed it last night."

"I'm sorry to hear that," Randy said. "I was afraid that something like that might have happened. Probably the same guy who took two cans of gas off the Ark."

"Any idea who the culprit might be?"

"One of the locals said Carlos Soto escaped last night from the jail. Could have been him."

"You're kidding. Carlos Soto was in jail here?"

"Yeah, you know him?" Randy said, apparently surprised that I might know the trouble-maker.

"Kind of."

"He's one of the island bad guys that they arrested in French Harbor for robbery. Since French Harbor doesn't have a jail, they sent him here till they could transfer him to the mainland. How do you know him?"

"It's like a nightmare. I caught him ripping off the yacht and now I can't seem to get rid of him. How did he escape?"

"It's just a one-room concrete block building, but he probably had some help. Wow, I thought he had robbed some local folks. I didn't know it was you."

"Yeah, we were the lucky ones. You have any idea where he took my whaler?"

"With that nice whaler and the gas he took from me, he's probably headed for the mainland. You know," Randy continued, "there has been some talk, nothing definite, you understand, that Carlos Soto and his cronies been looking for something definite. Not sure, but something very big, maybe treasure. Who knows, they could have come into some information that has them very, very, interested in the waters off Roatan Island. There's always rumors among the local natives that we outsiders never hear. They seem to find the money to finance their adventures from what they can steal from outsiders, or the wealthy folks who live here.

"Many of the thieves here move to the mainland, or a few even to the U.S. where they have more to pick from. But not Carlos and his guys. They seem to never get very far from here. They *are* looking for something! I think they'll stay close or at least not be gone long. Only my hunch, you understand, but I doubt you'll ever see your whaler again."

"I'll still need to report it."

"Heavens, yes. Anything I can do to help?"

Grateful for the offer for assistance from my new friend, I returned to the task of inflating the spare boat. We had the Avon putting along in less than an hour. The small Yamaha was running smooth and true. Though it wasn't much for speed, it was safe and dependable. At least until we could get back home to order a new whaler from the States, it would serve as a way to get ashore without swimming. We could not get very close to shore without running aground, due to Magic's deep hull.

"Here's Burt's. Why don't we see if he has any ideas?" Randy suggested.

We pulled up in front of the ice plant where the launch would be out of the way and planned to see if Burt was in his office on the second floor above the general store. Before we had time to do more than make the Avon fast and step on dock, Burt came around the corner of the store.

"Good morning," he said, glancing at the Avon and the small Yamaha engine. "You've come down in the world since last night. Where's your whaler?"

"I wish I knew," I said. Before I had a chance to say much more, Randy blurted out about the cut line, missing gas, and Carlos Soto.

"Old Carlos was busy, I guess. The store was hit too last night: three pistols, some ammo, and a bunch of canned goods. I guess they took all they could carry. I've already been on the radio to Coxen Hole and French Harbor; but with your whaler and Randy's gas, I'd better try to radio La Ceiba on the mainland."

"That's where I figured he went," Randy volunteered.

"Yeah, he's too well known here on the island to stay around long, and, unless I miss my guess, Zep's involved in there somewhere. So, they're looking for him too."

"The sea was smooth as glass last night," I added.

"He's headed for mainland, all right," Randy repeated.

"Too bad the sea wasn't running. He would have been forced to stay around the island, but he's probably headed for the mainland," Burt agreed. "Why don't you fellows come up for some coffee while I try to raise the port captain over at La Ceiba? He'll need a good description of your whaler, Jim, so you need to be there when I radio.

"You fellows pull up a chair and make yourselves at home." He showed us to his office and indicated the chairs. He yelled downstairs to a slender black girl who was leaning against the door frame to bring up a pot of coffee. Closing the door, he crossed the room to where the radios were located.

Burt's office view was impressive. The windows along one wall of the large room overlooked the narrow strip of land between the canal and the ocean. The room had that earthy-island smell common in tropical environments, mixed with aroma of coffee beans and cigar smoke. A large oak desk piled high with papers gave the room an "office" look. A well-marked wooden swivel chair stood between the desk and the wall of windows. Randy and I each picked one of the two captain-type arm chairs that faced the desk and took a seat. A large maroon over-stuffed couch that had seen some use stood behind us, covering half of the back wall. We watched as Burt fiddled with one of the several marine and ham radio set-ups that covered a long table at the far end of the office underneath a large colorful map of the Bay Islands.

"La Ceiba Puerto Authorities. La Ceiba Puerto Authorities. This is Blue Water Azul, Oak Ridge, Roatan," Burt repeated several times before the radio crackled to life.

"This is La Ceiba Puerto Authorities to Blue Water Azul. Go ahead, Oak Ridge. I read you loud and clear, Burt." The radio operator, Lieutenant Reyes, obviously knew him. Burt began to recount the events of the previous night. He explained briefly that the theft of the launch and gas led him to believe that the escaped thief was headed their way. He confirmed that he had also notified Coxen Hole and French Harbor to cover those possibilities. Burt warned La Ceiba about the theft of the weapons and ammunition to make them aware that Carlos Soto and his accomplices were armed.

Reyes promised to inform the Port Captain and the La Ceiba police immediately and asked for a description of the launch and motor. Burt put me on the radio and I identified myself as the captain and owner of Magic. Giving the documentation number and other relevant information, I informed the lieutenant of our clearing customs in the Bay Islands at Coxen Hole, and that we were on a pleasure cruise of unknown duration. After this was completed, I described the whaler in detail.

When the lieutenant asked for the serial number, I explained that though I didn't know the number from memory, I did have it aboard Magic. I doubted that there were many new Whalers in La Ceiba equipped with twenty-five horse-powered Evinrudes with "Tender of Magic" painted on the bow and stern. Honduras has several hundred kilometers of shore line, and the launch could be anywhere. The lieutenant insisted that he needed the numbers for his report in case the launch turned up. I promised to send the numbers back on my return to the yacht and handed the microphone to Burt, who verified he would radio the numbers to La Ceiba.

Signing off, Burt looked up to see the slender girl standing in the doorway with a tray containing coffee, cups, sugar, cream, and several sugar tarts of the island variety. "You might as well stay for coffee," he said. He took the tray and dismissed her, then poured the coffee as we took our seats around the desk.

Burt sat back in his swivel chair and sipped his coffee. "I don't know what you've heard about Honduras, so let me fill you in some. They pretty much leave us alone out here in the Bay Islands, almost like we were a separate country. We like it that way. I'm telling you this so you don't hold out too much hope of getting your launch or motor back. I don't believe they'll find it, but even if they did, you'd probably never hear of it. Some army officer or policeman will paint over the name and it will be theirs."

"You're probably right, Burt. I don't really expect to see it again, but I do want to go through the motions."

"Well, if I can be of service, don't hesitate to ask."

"I appreciate it, but my Avon inflatable should serve my purpose until I can replace the whaler. I just hope I've seen and heard the last of Mr. Soto. He's beginning to head my shit list."

"Well, I hope so too," Burt replied.

Randy promised to get the numbers when we returned to Magic and see that Burt received them, so that he could pass them on to Lieutenant Reyes.

"I'd be glad to relay the numbers," Burt said. "Maybe I'll see you and your pretty wife later on at the Happy Landing."

"Probably not. We most likely will put to sea around midday."

"Why so soon?" Randy asked.

"We're down to our last dingy and so far the peace and quiet of the Bay Islands hasn't quite reached our expectations, so we'd best move on."

"Where you headed?" Burt asked.

"We're not sure yet, but after this morning, Tobi said she'd had enough. I can't blame her. Maybe she'll have an idea when I get back."

When Randy and I started our return to the yacht, Tobi watched from the deck. When the Avon was within hailing distance, she appeared anxious to find out what we'd discovered.

"Any luck on the whaler?" she yelled.

"Sorry, looks like we'll have to write it off."

After the inflatable was strung off the stern, Randy joined us in the stern cockpit while I filled her in on our conversation with Burt and Lieutenant Reyes from the mainland.

"Well, it's about what I expected. I guess the Avon will have to do. Besides, I kinda like the little guy. Reminds me of when we were poor in the Bahamas."

"Are you still wanting to leave today?" I asked.

"More than ever. I've had enough of this kind of excitement," she answered.

While Tobi went below to hunt for the serial numbers of whaler and motor, Randy questioned me about our destination.

"Just head east I guess. We have to stop at the Island of Guanaja to clear customs for the Bay Islands, then maybe we'll run down the Mosquito Coast of Nicaragua or to the Sand Blast Islands off Panama. We really haven't had much time to discuss it, and we usually make our cruising itinerary a joint decision."

Tobi returned with the serial numbers written on a piece of paper and handed it to Randy. He promised to keep an eye out for our whaler and said he'd visit our ranch over in Rio Dulce if he ever had the opportunity.

I watched the aluminum launch head for shore, then turned my attention to Tobi. "I'll pull the Avon up on the davits, if you'll fix lunch."

"Already have. Peanut butter sandwiches. They're fast, easy to fix, easy to clean up. I like them, and you had better act like they're just what you wanted."

I decided I better love peanut butter sandwiches.

As we finished, I asked the question that had been hanging unspoken between us. "Where do you want to go?"

"Just away from here and these thieving natives. Let's just put to sea and find us some privacy. Okay?"

"Best idea I've heard all day."

CHAPTER 7

After I did a few chores, the anchor came up and was secured in its cradle. Tobi and I were heading through the Oak Ridge channel a few minutes past noon. The weather was bright and sunny, but the breeze was a little stiff for real comfort. After clearing the cut, I steered east. I raised the genny sail and Magic dug in. The boat loved running in a stiff breeze like the day offered. Continuing on an easterly course, we stayed a mile or so off the southern coast of Roatan Island with just the large genny sail up. We were making about seven knots. More sail would have increased our speed, but not much, and we would have paid the price in comfort. Taking out the chart, Tobi spread it over the outside cocktail table and weighted the corners down with a pair of binoculars and several books that were handy. I studied it for a while.

"We should clear the east end of Roatan before it gets dark. Then, the only place between there and Guanaja is Mary's Island that's about fifteen miles east of Roatan. We shouldn't try to make port in Guanaja at night. So we need to look for a nice cove toward the end of the island, or we'll have to spend several hours tonight tacking offshore near Guanaja waiting for first light. What do you think, Tobi?"

"If we hold off at sea tonight, we won't get any sleep. I'd rather find a good anchorage near the tip of the island. Then we can relax tonight and make a day sail to Guanaja tomorrow and clear customs out on the same day," she suggested.

I thought for a second. "After Guanaja, we should be able to run south on autopilot with the radar alarm on during the night, so we can sleep. Sounds good to me. You watch the shore for a nice anchorage, and we'll head in if the island chart says there's enough depth."

Three hours later, I was stretched out on the aft deck cushions with the auto steering engaged, my thoughts miles away.

"Oh, Jim, look," Tobi said excitedly.

"What? What's up?" I asked, returning to the present.

"Over there," she replied, poking a pair of binoculars in my direction. "Isn't that bay the most lovely place you've ever seen?"

I squinted through the glasses. About three quarters of mile off the port bow was a cove so picturesque it could have been right out of a travelogue. The water was a deep blue and the surrounding hills on three sides were several hundred feet high, covered with a heavy growth of dark emerald green. There was a narrow strip of white sandy beach along the back of the cove and no sign of life. Perfect.

"Looks great, but there's a lot of white water at the entrance. Let's have a look at the chart."

After a few minutes studying the chart and checking our position on the Sat Nav, I looked up. "No problem getting in there. That's Old Port Royal!"

"Wow, I can see why that couple fell in love with this place. It's beautiful. Oh, Jim, I don't care if it is haunted. I'd always regret it if we don't stop there. Do you mind?"

"Looks fantastic to me. After French Harbor and Oak Ridge, I'd prefer a few friendly ghosts to some of the live locals we've run into."

I turned the wheel a few points to the north to bring us close to shore as I angled toward the haunted cove. Guarded by three small rocky cays perched above the reef that ran the length of the harbor mouth, the paradise was well protected. The cays, standing fifteen to twenty feet above water, were covered with a tangled, scrubby growth that clung to the rocky surface. The barrier reef broke at the eastern and western end of the bay, and both openings appeared to be at least sixty foot wide with plenty of depth for deep-draft boats to enter.

We came abreast of the first opening in the reef and just looked, then went for the channel at the eastern end. I dropped the genny while Tobi started the diesel. As I lined up on the channel, I watched the fathomer rise from a depth of two-hundred feet to forty-five feet over a distance of approximately a hundred and fifty yards before the digital reading leveled off and held at forty-five feet. A few short minutes later, we passed through the cut into the harbor of Old Port Royal.

The difference was amazing. Leaving a four to six foot sea running outside the reef, the inside was like entering a smooth mill pond. It was easy to see why this was a favored shelter. With the high hills on three sides and the protection of Fowler Reef and the three rocky cays from the sea, a ship could wait out some heavy weather in this harbor.

"This is the place we've been looking for," Tobi said, smiling from ear to ear. "I'm even glad it has a bad reputation. Maybe we can have it all to ourselves. Honey, let's not leave here tomorrow. We can do like we planned before we left home, and just dive and play together until we have our fill. As long as we're careful, we can even look the face of the reef over good. Of course, if it seems too rough down below or we get bad vibes, we can just pack it in. What do you say? All right?"

"Slow down. You're the one who wanted to get the hell out of Bay Island this morning."

"A girl has the right to change her mind, and, besides, that was before I saw Port Royal. I just love this place and I have a lucky feeling about it. Please. Let's stay and explore awhile. Okay?"

"So far it looks fine, but if I don't like the looks of the face of the reef from the ocean side, we pack it in, like you said. No arguments."

"Okay, Captain, you're the boss on the dive," she consented. She continued looking around the idyllic cove.

"Where do you want to drop the hook? The whole place looks perfect."

"Let's try more towards the back of the bay. With the hills and trees in the background, Magic will be harder to see from seaward. I'd like to try and keep this place all to ourselves."

I eased the yacht in until we were about two hundred yards from shore with the depth meter recording forty feet of water under the sensor. Ten minutes later, the anchor was set and we were smiling at each other across the cocktail table in the aft cockpit. At almost five o'clock, we were only thirty miles up the coast from Oak Ridge, even though it seemed we had traveled light years away from the settlements and trouble. Cruising people search for these places that appear to be from another era.

After we had settled down for a while, I agreed to hang the Hibachi off the rail while Tobi started thawing three big steaks to make up for the earlier peanut butter sandwiches that I had sworn I loved. As we relaxed on the stern deck cushions, sipping chilled wine while juicy steaks sizzled on the Hibachi, we let the gentle motion of the boat at anchor rock us while we waited for the steaks to cook.

Coco and Peanut, having been aboard since French Harbor, were starting to get anxious, as we listened to the howler monkeys on shore warning the area that strangers were near.

"Here, you two," Tobi said, cutting the third steak into small pieces. Her good mood evidently extended to the dogs, resulting in an unexpected treat. Coco gulped her share down so that she could help Peanut eat his.

It was hard for me to imagine the tragic history that this bay had experienced in the distant and not so distant past. All the suffering and misery that the numerous pirates' prisoners must have experienced during the years that the fearsome frigates bearing the skull and crossbones controlled these waters. Then, to remember the horrifying story of the couple who had invested their dreams, money, and hard work trying to develop and share this small corner of paradise with others, only for one to meet death and the other to survive a fate worse than death.

"Your plate's ready. Do you want to eat up here or in the dining area below?"

"Up here would suit me just fine."

"Good. If you'll dump the charcoal overboard, I'll bring everything up here."

As we enjoyed steaks that would rival those from the Embers in Miami Beach, I decided we were fortunate to have stopped in Port Royal and learned of this private destination. I would be even happier if the rumors kept it so private that we would fail to see another soul until we were homeward bound.

"I have a lucky feeling about this place," Tobi repeated. "And I had really wanted to explore Fowler Reef."

"We'll give it a good looking over, but remember, I don't want you out of my sight until I'm comfortable with the face of that reef."

"Don't worry. I'll stick to you like glue, even though I'm pretty good in the water myself."

"I realize that. You're pretty good at sticking with anything you put your mind to. It's just the unexpected things that can get a person in trouble, no matter how good they are. Besides, Baby, you know I love you so much that it makes me afraid."

"Afraid of what?"

"You know, losing you."

"Why would you ever worry about losing me when you've had me around for so long?" You know I wouldn't trade you for a farm in Texas, or anything else I can think of. Heck, you couldn't even run me off if you tried. You're stuck with me for the duration. That's probably why you married an orphan in the first place. I haven't anywhere to run to."

I hesitated before I went on. "I don't mean losing you that way. It's just that I feel so damn lucky to have the hand we were dealt, that I get worried that an accident, or something unforeseen, might separate us."

"Jim, don't even think like that. We'll be old and gray sitting in our rocking chairs one of these days, holding hands while we relive our experiences and our memories. And that time will come soon enough, so no more morbid thoughts. Just live and love every day for itself and be thankful that we have each other. And if you help me clear up the dishes and galley, I might even let you get fresh with me!"

"You talked me into that deal. But this time, let's put Coco and Peanut in the bathroom, so they don't join us."

In about fifteen minutes, I had my teeth brushed and a little Habit Rouge sprayed in all the right places. Grabbing a bottle of Napoleon Cognac and two tumblers, I whistled my way out on deck. Bringing several large pillows from the day salon below, Tobi was already busy on the aft deck, building herself a nest on the deck cushions under the aft rail near where the little Avon inflatable still hung on the boat davits.

I watched her for a few moments and felt the tenderness wash over me. I knew that I was one of the luckiest men in the world to have married this girl-woman when she was just eighteen years of age.

When I had first met her, she was an orphan. Her parents, having been killed in an accident a year earlier, had left her on her own and all alone. I was twenty-seven and reasonably successful for a man of that age as a pilot for the Ozark Airlines. Owning a small apartment complex with a large note attached, I was satisfied that my roads were soon to be paved with gold. Unmarried, I fully intended to stay that way, at least in the foreseeable future. But while Christmas shopping in downtown St. Louis, I had wandered into the toy department of the Famous-Barr store. Wanting a unique present for my new nephew, I wasn't really sure what I was looking for.

As a clerk in the store, Tobi had watched me examining all the toys. "Can I help you?" she had asked.

I looked up and laid eyes on Tobi for the first time. She was five foot six inches tall, weighed about a hundred and twenty pounds, and had long thick blond hair cascading down to just past her shoulders. She had sparkling grey-green eyes, the prettiest teeth a person would wish for, and a figure that Cole of California would love for its bathing suits. Her voice was so engaging that it had me fumbling around for ways to keep her talking. She helped me choose a gray furry donkey that was large enough for a child to ride on. Sporting a red saddle and long soft ears, it was mounted on rollers to allow the rider to push or pull it about. I knew it was exactly what I wanted for my nephew, Tabby. Perfect!

But by this time, Tabby was becoming a lot less important to me, while this girl-woman was becoming a lot more so. I was lost, and we were married six months later. I had been pinching myself ever since just to be sure I wasn't dreaming. Over the last twenty years, she had followed me all over the world while I pursued various flying jobs in more places than I cared to remember. She had always been there with a smile, good will, and never-ending work and support for all my endeavors. All these thoughts went through my mind as I watched her building her nest on the deck of our sailboat in this beautiful corner of the earth.

"Well, Handsome, I thought you weren't going to show up," she said. She turned to see me standing with cognac in hand. "And you even brought a present!"

Bending, I gave her a quick kiss and eased myself down beside her on the deck cushions. She took the tumblers and cognac and poured the drinks. Then we settled back against the large pillow Tobi had arranged on deck for that purpose. I could smell the Estee Lauder perfume that she had added since our parting after dinner a few minutes earlier.

"Here's to us, Tobi. May we never be parted."

"I'll drink to that, Darling," she said, reaching with her free hand to caress my neck and ear.

Impelled by mutual impulses, we set our drinks aside and embraced as we slid further down on the cushions. Our kisses were as hot and as passionate as

they had been on our wedding night, twenty years
earlier. Tobi hadn't aged, only matured, and had grown
more beautiful through the years. As our tongues met
and our saliva mixed, our breath grew hot. I ran my
hand under her T-shirt and caressed her perfectly
formed breast and felt the nipple harden and rise against
my hand. She ran her hand down my chest to the front
of my shorts to undo my top button with practiced ease.
As the zipper slid down almost of its own accord, she
slipped her hand inside my shorts and began fondling
my erection.

I removed my hand from her breast and lifted the T-
shirt over her head as she continued to hold me.
Admiring her beautiful body, I kissed my way down to
her right breast and began to tease the nipple with my
tongue. Putting her free hand behind my head, she
caressed my head in tempo with the hand softly
stroking my penis. As I eased my hand inside her
panties, she began to purr like a kitten with soft mewing
sounds laced with urgent whispers.

She squirmed, trying to wiggle out of her clothes
without interrupting the moment. As her movements
became more urgent, her shorts and panties slid easily
over her firm-rounded buttocks and past her knees. She
raised her legs high to make it easy to slip them over
her bare feet. This obstacle over, I began to stroke her
softly, sliding my finger expertly over her clitoris, while
she pushed my head to the other breast and continued
until we could not hold it any longer. She helped me
remove my Levi shorts and we made love on the deck
cushions under a full moon with millions of stars

twinkling their delight as we took our mortal pleasures there in that private place with all the heavens looking on.

Our passions spent, we lay on deck in each other's arms for more than hour, enjoying the familiar touch of our bodies. I would have been willing to spend the entire night on deck, but the wind began to pick up speed, gathering a few clouds from there and here and hurrying them across the sky. I could hear the wind singing through the stainless-steel rigging of Magic's main mast about sixty feet above the deck.

"That wind is going to blow us in some rain tonight," I said.

"I was thinking the same thing. I hate to go below, it's so comfy up here, but I think we had better," she said as she began to gather clothes and brandy off the deck.

"You go on down, I just want to check the anchor and brake before I come below."

"I love you."

"I love you, too," I answered as I padded forward— bare footed and naked as the day I was born—to check the anchor. This complete, I entered the pilot house and glanced at the wind indicator and barometer. The barometer had slowly fallen, but only down a couple of points since we had anchored. The wind had begun to kick up its heels, measuring a steady thirty knots with an occasional gust to forty or so. There should be no problem for us in this vessel, especially in a sheltered anchorage like Old Port Royal. I was glad we had ducked in here instead of making for Guanaja and lying off shore that night. It would have been very uncomfortable. In a short length of time, a wind of this nature could raise some monster waves in open water.

I returned on deck and closed all the rain shutters. They would keep out all but a very heavy blowing rain, even with the windows open. But if we closed the windows, it would become necessary to run the air-conditioner, which, in turn, would make it necessary to run the generator. Usually, it was only advisable to run the air-conditioner in dire emergencies or when dock-side power was not available.

I shivered slightly, only for a second. Maybe it was because things seemed almost too perfect that had caused the fleeting unease. So many things can go wrong in a seemingly perfect life in a near perfect setting. Natural hazards, accidents, man-made danger, so many possibilities. I shrugged the feeling off and went below. It's not that we had anything to fear in this peaceful cove.

Down below, Tobi was in her starboard berth in the main salon. Fast asleep, she was curled up on her right side with her arm around her two small dogs. Looking as contented as she, they were awake and watching my every move. Turning off Tobi's reading light, I fell into the other berth. After saying a quick prayer of thanks, I soon fell asleep to the soothing hum of the air conditioner, oblivious to any indication of approaching danger.

CHAPTER 8

After a person spends considerable time on a vessel, he becomes attuned to the moods of the ship, geared to the change in weather. Having spent a lot of time on my yacht, I was awakened by the boat tugging on its anchor. I glanced at my watch's luminous dial. One-thirty. I arose and stepped up into the pilot house. I could see the rain slanting down in sheets through the narrow slits of the rain shutter as the northeasterly wind howled a mournful tune through the top rigging. Magic had her anchor chain pulled taunt and had swung around—bow to the wind and stern to seaward. Gazing at the wind vane indicator on the bulkhead, I could see the gauge playing back and forth between forty-five and fifty-five knots with frequent gusts.

I sat at the chart table and tuned the single-side-band to one of the all-weather channels for marine weather out of Miami. The reception was good despite the high hills of Roatan that were now in front of us. The station went through the weather for this hemisphere, quadrant by quadrant, until they finally reached that section of the Caribbean, about sixteen degrees latitude. Though the forecast was not good, I had heard a lot worse in days gone by. We were in the grip of a mild norther and small craft advisories were in effect for our area. The sea was expected to be fifteen to twenty feet with winds to fifty-five knots out of the north, northeast, with higher winds in the squall area.

Locally, heavy rains were forecast. I flipped the radio off and watched the rain coming through the shutters. *They were right on the button there*, I thought. I thanked my lucky stars that we had decided to stop in the sheltered bay. If we had been at sea that night, we would have had a rough ride, but in this weather, we could not have found a better place to hole up. I took one last look through the shutters and crept back to bed. Tobi and her pets were sleeping peacefully.

At seven-thirty the next morning, the smell of coffee brewing and the clatter of dishes from the galley brought me from my slumber.

"Wake up, Sleepy Head," she called from the gallery. "It's a yucky day outside, but I'm in a good mood and lonesome. Get up and keep me company, and I'll feed you a good breakfast."

Liking the sound of that deal, I threw myself out of my bunk and into a pair of shorts. Slipping on my topsiders, I ducked into the galley and gave Tobi a kiss.

"Go on up and have a seat. The table's set and breakfast will be served in five minutes."

As we sat enjoying our breakfast, Tobi inquired as to the Captain's agenda for the day. Raising the rain shutters on the starboard window, I stared out through the cut to the sea. The wind had slackened during the early morning, but was still out of the northeast at a respectable twenty knots, leaving the waves at a monstrous level. They were pounding the reef and the three rocky cays with tremendous force. The salt spray drifted forty feet above the entrance to Port Royal. Though the rain had played itself out, a light drizzle continued to fall with an overcast sky. Tobi had described it perfectly—a yucky day.

"Well, I don't know of anything important for today. I'm just glad we were anchored here instead of getting our brains beaten out on the open sea."

"When do you think we can do any diving?"

"Probably not for at least two days. The sea will stay up awhile after this blow. We can catch the marine weather on the radio, then I want to do some more calculations on the tide tables here and around the Bahama Bank. So you can either help me on the calculations, read or watch a video, or just be lazy."

"I hope the rain stops," she said.

"If it does, we'll let the Avon down and poke around the edge of the bay. Maybe even see if anything's left of the marina the boating couple started."

"Good. I'd like to get out and I know Coco and Peanut could use some time ashore. As long as there are no people or other dogs they could run and play awhile."

While Tobi cleared the remains of breakfast, I located the large scale chart of the area and my marine almanac and started working on the tide changes for that latitude. On her way back down to the galley, Tobi adjusted the dial on the radio. The marine weather broadcast was loud and clear. The norther and related squalls were reported to have moved to the west. Small-craft advisories remained in effect due to high seas. I realized the worst was over and the sea would return to three to five feet in a couple of days. We would probably be able to do some diving on the outside of the reef by then.

I toyed with the tide calculations for the majority of the morning until I had the times and flow committed to memory. Tobi stuck around until she became bored, then she retired downstairs with a book. It was almost noon before the rain ceased, but dark clouds filled the sky and continued to drift across the horizon, leaving it overcast with no sign of the sun.

"How about lunch, Captain?" she asked, returning to the pilot house from below.

"Sounds good to me. I'm finished calculating, and, if my theory's right, we should be able to do our underwater exploring from early morning until about two in the afternoon. The tide starts to run about two forty-five, and any underwater turbulence created by the falling tide would begin around then. I think we'll be okay, as long as we give ourselves at least an hour before then for a good safe margin."

"Okay. Now all we have to worry about is the sea going down and the weather clearing up before the puppies and I get cabin fever. I hope you like sandwiches, because soup and sandwiches are all that's on the menu on rainy days." Her tone allowed for no disagreement.

"That's fine with me."

"Now that that's settled, would you mind letting the launch down after lunch? I'd like to go ashore with the dogs and let them run and play awhile."

By one-thirty, the whole family was seated in the little rubber Avon and headed for the strip of white sandy beach towards the rear of the bay. In a few minutes, we were dragging the launch onto the smooth sand.

Coco and Peanut, anxious to be about their business of exploring were first ashore. Walking hand in hand up the beach, Tobi and I allowed the dogs to run ahead of us. As Coco and Peanut reached the edge of the timber that surrounded the beach, they began to bark furiously at something that excited them. Concerned, Tobi and I broke into a trot until we came to the edge of the foliage and could see what was causing their excitement. The canines had managed to corner an iguana lizard about three feet long and it was a Mexican stand-off. The dogs didn't quite know what to do about the giant lizard, and the cornered creature was in the same situation. He couldn't quite comprehend the noisy little strangers invading his turf and creating such a ruckus.

Tobi and I laughed in relief and managed to call the dogs off while the lizard hurried deeper into the foliage with a relieved demeanor. Jumping and scampering around us, the puppies wanted praise for their discovery and bravery. We petted and bragged on them until the dogs were anxious to be off again.

At the far edge of the beach, we could see a sort of wooden structure protruding into the water. It had weathered until it was the same color as the trees and bushes in the background.

"Look, I bet that's the end of the dock that the boating couple built. Let's go see. Want to?" Tobi asked.

"Sure, we may as well have a look—the dogs are nearly there already." A little farther up the beach, Tobi and I easily identified the dock. It appeared solid and was connected to a building surrounded by brush and foliage that had crept around attempting to reclaim what was once theirs. We approached the end of the dock. Well-made of heavy timber, it had been treated with a type of petroleum product to give it a dark brown, almost black, appearance. I noticed the cross-braces had been drilled and connected with galvanized bolts. A lot of effort had been spent to construct this dock. The builders had intended for it to last many years.

We climbed upon the dock end from our edge of the beach. About four feet above ground level, it led to a large thirty foot by thirty foot structure that was made of the same treated wood as the dock, making it almost invisible against the dark shaded background and heavy foliage of the surrounding area. Several large openings were apparently meant to be windows, but hadn't received any glass or it had been taken by the ravage of time.

We looked through the large opening in front. Against the wall, a wooden stairway led up to a half-loft. Evidence of animal use was abundant throughout the building. We could see our small dogs rummaging around inside, investigating everything.

"Not much left to see. Kinda sad. That couple must have worked hard to make their private dream come true. It's a shame it was stamped out in such tragic manner," Tobi said. "I can almost see the harbor full of cruising yachts and boaters stopping here for a few days in their wanderings."

"Yeah, it's strange how one event can alter the course of things so drastically. Just think, if it hadn't been for the tragic end met by the couple building this place, how different it would be today."

"I see what you mean."

"But in a few short years the bush will have completely reclaimed this place. There will be no sign of their having passed this place. Let's go back to the launch," she said.

"I get a sad feeling here. It's as if I can feel the force of the wasted dreams."

"Okay. I'm ready. Not much left to see anyway and the dogs have finished their exploration."

As I finished my statement, the dogs began making barking, growling, and excited exploring sounds near the back of the now deserted, unfinished building. I called to them to quiet themselves and come on. They only increased the volume of the racket.

I said, "We'd better see what has them so worked up." We headed deeper into the building, angling toward the back corner where the dogs were still in full voice. We could see evidence of some recent visitors. There was an area where soil had been dumped on the wood flooring. Small stones strewn about created a crude insulation between the floor and a rustic fire pit lined with stones. This was certainly created by humans. There was a circle of larger stones ringing it, with evidence of a fire having burned in the stone circle in the not-too-distant past. We looked at each other and began looking around. There were several rum bottles strewn around the area.

Tobi said, "Hmm, maybe a wild party we missed?"

I picked up a small stick about five inches long and began raking something out of the trash litter. On closer examination, we saw it was a chicken with the head missing. It was only a dead chicken, but it sure excited the dogs, and I could feel goose bumps begin to tickle my body.

Tobi suddenly said, "Jim, look here." She was holding a metal can that had been fashioned crudely into a cup.

I looked inside the cup and found what appeared to be dried blood. I touched it lightly with my finger and a deep rust colored film transferred to my finger from the cup. We looked at each other wide eyed and Tobi said, "Remind you of another place?"

I answered softly, "Haiti. Voodoo." It brought back memories of the island nation we had spent time on while studying the national religion of Haiti years before.

Tobi said, "It gives me a feeling of unease. Headless chicken, rum, blood rituals, spells, and superstition. I believe there is a similar belief called 'Santeria' in the islands that has blood rituals and sacrifice as part of their beliefs."

I said, "Even our private cove may not be as private as we had thought."

Tobi replied, "Let's get out of here and back aboard Magic where we don't feel spooked or violated and talk about this over a stiff drink.

We made our way back to the beach and the launch. Though there was still an overcast sky, the wind had slackened even further to a moderate breeze. But glancing past where Magic was anchored to the entrance of Port Royal Harbor, it was evident that the sea was still plenty rough. As we pushed the Avon into the water, we could see the waves rolling in and crashing on Fowler reef, casting a heavy spray towards the heavens.

Coco and Peanut, anxious to return, had been the first aboard the Avon. I stood in knee-deep water, holding it steady until Tobi climbed aboard and seated herself. I hoisted myself inside and started the little Yamaha engine and headed back to Magic.

Once back aboard Magic, I decided to haul the Avon back up on the davits, the memory of the cut rope and lost whaler still fresh on my mind. Checking the anchor and taking a look around the yacht, I could find nothing that demanded my attention, so I made my way aft where Tobi and the dogs made a welcome sight. She was seated next to the large varnished wheel with her small amber Pomeranian on one side, watching her and me alternatively, intuitively as if waiting for a command. Her champagne-colored toy poodle waited on her other flank in the same posture and attitude. Even though both dogs were very small, they had as much of the protective determination toward Tobi as that of the fiercest breed you could name.

"I sure have a fine crew aboard," I said, smiling my approval. "The yacht looks ship-shape to me, so maybe we could all reward ourselves with a nap."

"I'm ready, Captain," she said, leading the way below.

She loaded a tape with a good soothing beat by the Judds on the tape-deck and kept the volume low while everyone stretched out on our bunks for a much-needed rest. With Tobi on the starboard couch with her snuggling companions and I on the portside couch, it didn't take long for the beat of the music and the pounding of sea on the reef in the background to lull everyone into a deep sleep.

CHAPTER 9

I came awake listening to the sounds around me, trying to identify what had disturbed my sleep. I opened my eyes slightly. Tobi was crying. Something must be seriously wrong, because she wasn't a girl who gave over to nervousness or hysterics easily. "What's wrong, Tobi?" I asked, seeing the big tears running down her cheeks.

"Something's wrong with little Peanut. His head is all swollen and he's burning up with fever."

I crossed the salon and lifted the small poodle. He was a little furry ball, his coat unclipped, soft, curly, and very thick. The dog felt warm and had been sweating, his head damp and matted from perspiration. His eyes, just small slits, had nearly been closed by the swelling. Looking at me from behind the tiny slits, he tried licking my hand. My heart went out to the little guy. Though Peanut was very sick, he was not whining or crying, just trying to be a little tough guy, putting all his trust in me. Coco was staring at us, anxious and worried about her little friend.

I didn't know much about treating animals, but we did live on a farm and had a library on animal treatment, though we usually depended on a vet for our needs. I did know that our small treasure was in mortal danger.

"Please, do something, Jim. I couldn't stand to lose my little Peanut. I love him so much."

"Take it easy, Tobi. Has he taken a fall or anything you know about?"

"No, nothing. He was just fine when we came back from ashore . . . and he was fine when we laid down for a nap. Coco woke me up a few minutes ago, licking my face and whining. I thought she had to go pee, but she was trying to tell me Peanut was sick. What's the matter with him?"

"I'm not sure. I thought maybe he'd taken a fall. It's almost like his neck was broken, but maybe with the swelling and all, he doesn't have the strength to hold it up." Peanut's head rolled back in my big hand for support."

"Can't we radio the mainland for a doctor or get an airplane here or something?"

"You don't know how much I wish we could, but even if I could reach La Ceiba, there's no chance of getting help. We'd be lucky to get Magic through the cut safely with the sea pounding that reef. I'm afraid we'd broach. And I'm sure that Peanut, in his condition, would be dead long before we could reach the mainland. No, we'll have to do our best here. Go and get our emergency medical kit and I'll try to find something."

"Don't let my Peanut . . ." She began to sob.

"Now, Tobi, stop crying and do like I asked. Don't count Peanut out yet. He's a tough little guy and I'll do my best." We had a fairly complete medical locker. Everything from morphine and syringes to several kinds of antibiotics and medicines for burns, breaks, and infections. There was Dramamine for sea sickness and everything else you would expect to find on a ship and more, but nothing for a dog. As Tobi went for the medicine box, I examined Peanut more thoroughly. I couldn't find any evidence of an external injury. Squinting at me with his liquid-brown eyes, trusting as ever, Peanut was just barely conscious.

"Peanut, my little friend, you're a very sick guy. I wish you could talk to me and tell me what happened." I began to play "what if" with myself. Could the headless chicken, voodoo, or whatever, crowd have anything to do with Peanut being ill? Could they have left something? Poison, natural herbs, or potions that would be harmful to people or animals? Anything? But they could not even know we're here. Or could they? No, my mind was playing tricks on me.

Peanut licked his dry nose and whined softly, as if he were trying to answer. I had to blink the tears back.

"Peanut, my friend, you don't have a very good chance, but just keep your faith in Tobi and I and we'll try for that miracle."

Tobi rushed across the salon lugging the heavy box containing all the ship's medicine.

"What do you think could have happened to him?" she asked.

"I can't find any sign of an external injury, so I'm going to guess he's been bitten somewhere on the face or head by a poisonous insect, spider, scorpion, or something like that."

"Do you think he could have been bitten by a snake while we were ashore?"

"It's possible, but I don't believe it was a snake. I think the dogs would have kicked up a ruckus about a snake. Remember the one they staged over the iguana? No, I really favor a spider, something he would have been unaware of until the poison started taking hold."

"What can we do? We have to do something."

"The only thing I can think of is to get some antibiotics into him. I don't know if they'll help, but we have to try. He's in real trouble."

I looked over the selection of antibiotics and settled on tetracycline caps. I handed three capsules to Tobi, who took them apart and shook the powder into two ounces of hot water. Allowing the powder to dissolve, we ruled against injecting the small dog with the mixture because of the difficulty in gauging dosage. We agreed to spoon-feed the antibiotic to him and save the syringe for a last resort.

Before trying the medication, I took a glass of cold water and a teaspoon and started spooning plain water into Peanut's mouth. The animal was parched and took the cool water a spoon at a time. He seemed grateful for the liquid and rewarded me with a look that appeared trustful. Tobi took the cup with the dissolved powder while I held Peanut's head and opened his mouth. She began spooning the liquid into him. Peanut didn't seem to like the antibiotic taste but was in no shape to complain much. In a few minutes, Tobi had given him the last drop of the potion.

Now, all we could do was wrap him in a comforter and let him sweat the poison out.

"That may help bring his fever down. We'll cut his doses down to one cap now and repeat it every two hours."

"I hope there's some improvement." Tobi was much calmer now that she had things to do—and a bit of hope. The most important of all: hope.

We continued the medicine and nursing duties throughout the evening and well into the night. While Tobi and I worked over Peanut, Coco sat patiently watching everything like a small furry bedside nurse. Peanut dozed fretfully off and on between doses. He didn't seem any worse, but we couldn't see any improvement either. Tobi kept asking anxiously whether the medicine was working and I kept answering, "So far so good."

We kept on keeping on. Then, around midnight, Peanut appeared to be resting less fretfully. Still sweating, but not as much, and his coat was beginning to dry out in places. Neither of us had any desire for sleep or food that night.

With nothing much to do except wait and worry over Peanut, we began to think aloud. Tobi said, "You remember how upset the dogs were when we were ashore in the area where the devil worshipers or voodoos were meeting, or whatever was going on? It was like they had left evil spirits behind to guard this place and the dogs sensed it. And we were to dumb or sophisticated to even think about it?

I replied, "Speak for yourself. Sometimes I'm not so sure. I sometimes even think spells are possible. It would explain a lot of things for me. Tobi, you think that through while I give Peanut his medicine.

As I finished giving him his latest dosage, my mind wandered back to the time about five years earlier when we had received Peanut as a gift. A German friend in Guatemala, Ricardo Remlie, who had a large meat packing company called the Astoria Packing Company, raised champion Rottweilers and toy poodles. I kept a nice boat named the No Virgin there at the dock on our farm much of the time and he spent a lot of time in our company when we were at La Dulce Vida.

I had mentioned that I was wanting a small friend for Coco, but had been unable to find a Pomeranian in Guatemala. Tobi had found Coco in Oklahoma City on a state-side trip to pick up a white bull terrier puppy that I had ordered from a breeder in the Oklahoma City area. Awaiting her return from picking up the bull terrier puppy and taking care of FAA business for me, a couple of my macho friends and I were at the airport anxiously watching for my new bull terrier, a breed that was very rare, if not non-existent, in Guatemala.

We stood in the viewing area above where passengers disembarked for customs at the International Airport in Guatemala City when we spotted Tobi's blond head—an easy task, since blondes were as scarce as bull terriers in Guatemala. She spotted us looking over the rail on the floor above her and held up a small plastic sky kennel, Coco had her small furry head through a hole on top of the kennel viewing Guatemala and its people for the first time.

One of the friends, Paco Azzari, an ex-Olympic athlete and ex-pro-wrestler, gave me a surprised look and exclaimed in Spanish, "Don Diego, I think someone has tricked Doña Tobi. That dog isn't a bull terrier."

Surprised as Paco, I answered adamantly, "Well, Paco, I'm sure she must know that's no bull terrier, but maybe Tuffy had to ride with the baggage or something and isn't off the plane yet."

Paco glanced skeptically at me and said, "I sure hope so."

When we met Tobi in front of the terminal, we learned that the long-promised Tuffy was too young to travel and would have to await her return in a month.

After that, we had looked for a companion for Coco, until one weekend, Ricardo arrived with a small toy poodle that became our friend Peanut. Tobi had dubbed him Napoleon Astoria. Napoleon for his French heritage and Astoria in honor of Ricardo's meat company. "Napoleon" soon proved too bulky for daily use and Peanut became his nickname. Peanut had grown to love his new home and had become very protective of Tobi and Coco, not wanting to let either out of his sight. Tobi and I had likewise grown to love Peanut equally.

CHAPTER 10

I was interrupted from my woolgathering by Tobi's much calmer voice. "Peanut is resting better now. Why don't you get some sleep while I stay up with him to continue his medication?"

"That's okay, Tobi, but I was just daydreaming. I'm not really tired. I'll just hang out with you awhile after I go topside to take a look around and stretch."

Climbing the stairs, I felt the coolness of the night up on deck. A light, moderate breeze brushed my cheek. There was no rain, but the cloud cover had the stars blocked from view. Here at anchor, the water was smooth, and even though I could still hear the pounding of the waves off the reef hidden by the darkness, the sound of the waves crashing on the rocks had lost some of its fury from before. I felt my way up to the bow and tested the tension on the anchor chain. It was fairly slack due to the lack of wind or current to stretch it out. I knew we were well anchored after the big Danforth anchor had dug in deep during the blow, but my actions were mainly habit.

Again, from habit, I glanced up at the sky once more: still cloudy with very little light to see by. I made my way back to the pilot house and glanced at the barometer. It was steady with the probability that there was no more bad weather for a while. The red tracking light of the Sat-Nav continued to pick up a navigation satellite every half hour or so. Even though it only confirmed our anchored position, I preferred to leave it working continually, especially since it used little current and had such a complicated memory.

I went on downstairs and Tobi looked up and said, "I think he's doing better. He still looks awful but he licked my hand when I gave him his medicine a few minutes ago."

"I sure don't know much about dog doctoring, but I think if he gets through the night without any set-backs that he will be over the hump."

She said, "I guess that's why I love you so. You always know what to do no matter what the situation is. You seem to always make the right decisions."

"Heck, that's why I called this boat Magic. Didn't I tell you?"

"I know you're only kidding me, but I'm really serious, Jim. You do always know what to do, and do it. I've never known any other person as decisive as you are."

"Maybe it's habit from all my years in a crop duster. You know, when you fly all day with your wheels in the weeds most of the time, you have to be pretty decisive or you had better find another line of work."

Tobi and I sat with Peanut the rest of the night, making small talk and taking comfort in being together. About dawn, the patient was definitely better. His head was still swollen to twice its normal size and his eyes remained as small slits, but he was able to drink water on his own and even had a few bites of Mighty Dog.

I told Tobi, "I can see plenty of improvement. I think we'll discontinue his antibiotics now. We have been giving him 'people doses' so let's don't push our luck. We'll just keep him quiet until the swelling goes down and let nature take over for us awhile."

"You stay with Peanut and I'll fix breakfast," Tobi replied. "I'm starved and I know you must be too."

I was, but I hadn't thought about it till then.

After breakfast, Peanut was sleeping and I was sure the fever was about gone. The canine hadn't improved much in the looks department, but I was beginning to believe he might pull through. But I knew he was still a long way from being back to normal. The sun was still trying to break through the cloud cover and I could see the breakers on the reef. They had diminished a lot during the night and the wind was very light.

"Well, Tobi, if Peanut continues to improve today and the wind doesn't kick up any more, we may be able to look the reef over tomorrow."

"Unless Peanut is a whole lot better than he is now I don't intend to leave him."

"Well, as always, you're right. We'll just have to see, but the sea is laying down pretty fast and by tomorrow it should be all right. But of course it depends on how Peanut is doing."

We both napped on and off most of the day. Peanut continued to drink lots of water and ate a few more bites of his Mighty Dog but was still off his feed and could barely stand on his own. He would drink his water lying down with Tobi holding his dish for him. Coco was still much in attendance, but even she was beginning to look relieved. By late afternoon, the clouds were breaking up and the sun was coming through about half the time.

By evening, Peanut was able to stand and even wanted to go up on deck for a few minutes. His head was still swelled terribly. It gave him a deformed look, but I was sure he was going to be all right. We had a light supper and by mutual agreement decided to go to bed shortly after sundown. Peanut was feeling much better even if he didn't look much different with his big head.

I slept soundly all night and woke to a bright sunshiny morning. I could see the sun shining into the cabin through the slits in the shutters. The sun was coming through the port side shutter, so that meant Magic had swung back around on her anchor and was bow out to the sea again. I sat up in the bunk and was greeted with a weak but pleasant bark from Tobi's berth. Peanut was sitting up on his haunches watching me, and he greeted me with a feeble bark. His head was still swollen, but I could even smile at that now that our pet was so obviously better.

I spoke. "Good morning, Peanut. You sure had me worried for a while there. Sure wish you could tell me about it."

He looked up as if he wanted to talk about it, but of course he couldn't.

Tobi stirred then and said, "Good morning, Captain." She saw Peanut sitting up and gave him a hug and whispered endearments. He returned her affection as best he could and Coco got in the act, wanting her share of affection also.

"Jim, I'm so glad to see Peanut doing so good, but he sure is funny looking," Tobi said and laughed out loud.

It was good to hear her laugh. She said, "The sun is out again so now everything is going to be all right."

She popped out of bed and said, "I'll get breakfast, but Peanut and Coco get theirs first, so you just be lazy while I get organized and do my bathroom stuff."

"Okay, you got a deal." But as soon as she disappeared into the bathroom I got up and went out on deck.

It was a beautiful morning, so quiet and peaceful and private. We could have been the last people on earth for the privacy of this harbor. I took a leak over the rail as I often did. I smiled and thought of Tobi. She always scolded me for relieving myself over the rail, but I always just told her she was jealous because nature had equipped her differently and she couldn't manage it. I made a round of the deck and looked over the bow pulpit at the entrance to Port Royal. The sea had diminished to three to four feet, which was about normal. I was thinking it would be a good day for a dive and a look at the face of Fowler Reef from the ocean side.

Just then, Tobi called out. "Jim! Breakfast is on whenever you're ready."

"I'm ready," I answered, and made my way back aft and into the pilot house where she had steaming mugs of coffee, scrambled eggs, refried beans, cheese, and Canadian bacon, toast and jelly all laid out.

After breakfast, I wandered around the boat looking for something to occupy myself with while Tobi straightened things below. I finally settled on the diving gear. I got out the Bauer Nova Compressor that I used to fill our scuba tanks and filled it with gasoline and checked the oil. I started it up and checked the pop-off valves to make sure they were working properly. I laid out the tanks and looked at the O-rings for wear, checked the diaphragms in the regulators, inspected the diving vests, and looked over the Velcro fasteners. We had gear enough on board to outfit seven divers, but seldom had anyone along, so it was really just extra gear for Tobi and me.

After I finished my self-imposed chores, I wandered back inside. Tobi was down in the main salon with Coco and Peanut. When I came in she said, "I think he's trying to smile at me but he's swelled up so bad he can't quite make it. But it's a good sign anyway. Well, Captain, what's up? I heard you stirring around up on deck."

"I was just checking the diving gear over. The sea is down to moderate swells and I'd like to get in the water for a while this afternoon. How about you?"

"Well, I'd like to, but it's too soon to leave Peanut. If he is still improving tomorrow I would love to, but not today. And I really don't want you diving alone."

"I won't go down the face of the reef, but I think I'll look around the top with mask and snorkel. Maybe shoot us a grouper or a snapper for supper."

"That would be nice for a change." She hesitated. "But be careful."

"No sweat," I said, and went up on deck.

CHAPTER 11

I gathered up my gear: Mask, snorkel, fins, and Sea Hornet Spear Gun. I slipped on a pair of diving boots with thick rubber soles just in case I had to walk on any coral rock, then added a pair of Sure Grip gloves and mesh game sack to my pile and placed them in the Avon before letting it down into the water. I pulled the inflatable launch around to the starboard rail so I could climb down easier. I was just getting settled in the launch when Tobi came up on deck and handed me an Icom VHF hand-held radio.

"Better take this. I'll turn on the ship radio to channel 18, that way you can call me if you are away more than one hour or so."

"Okay, thanks." I took the radio and slipped it in a side pocket on the inflatable boat.

I started the little Yamaha engine and eased past Magic toward the entrance to the harbor. I had decided to leave the launch on the inside of the bay out of the swells, so I took aim at the inside shore of the largest of the three rocky cays guarding the harbor entrance. The shore was rocky and rough, but the water shoaled up to about two feet. I eased up to the shore and cut the engine. I found a strong plantlike bush clinging to the rocky surface of the cay, and after several healthy tugs decided it would be strong enough to hold the dingy. I made the bow line fast to the bush with enough slack for me to push the launch back out a few feet from the shore, and threw out a small stern anchor to keep it from drifting back against the rocky edge while I was away. I gathered up my gear again and picked my way across the rock to the ocean side, a short distance, probably 50 or 60 feet.

The sea was rolling in on this side in gentle swells. Not large, but enough that I was glad I had left the launch on the enclosed side. It would have taken a beating against the shore on this side. I sat down on a flat rock and put my mask with the snorkel attached on top of my head. I slipped on the power fins over my diving boots, tied the game bag to my web belt, put on my gloves, picked up my spear gun, and stepped into the water.

The water there went from waist deep to about 15 feet in just a few feet, so I leaned forward in the water, mostly submerged with my snorkel tip above the water. I had a good view of the bottom. The water was crystal clear and the surface swells had little effect below the surface. The bottom was rocky and rugged with little evidence of live coral. The bottom had numerous sea fans waving their colored leaves back and forth to their own tune.

There were thousands of small fish going about their business of survival. They looked like so many circus performers, all brightly done up in their stripes and spots and numerous colors. The only fish of any size in view were several parrot fish of about three or four pounds. They looked exactly like their name. Their large green and blue bodies and black protruding mouths instantly brought a parrot to mind. Their food value is very poor, so I ignored these and kicked my way over the rocky bottom toward the seaward edge of Fowler Reef.

The rocky bottom began to get farther away from me in my semi-submerged position on the surface. The depth went from 15 feet to 25 or 30 feet below me. But I was rewarded with much more abundant sea life. The fish were larger and I could see bright red patches of fire coral in several places below me. I watched a school of black and white spade fish chase each other around their undersea world for a few minutes. Then a school of zebra fish caught my eye as they raced past beneath me.

I spotted a red colored hog snapper farther out toward the edge of the reef. He was about 10 pounds with his high spike fin fanned out. His food value is rated very good, so I kicked my way seaward in his general direction. Before I arrived at the place where I had spotted him, he had disappeared over the edge of the reef. I continued on at a leisurely pace in that general direction anyway.

As I neared the edge of the reef, I could see the different shades of the water that had passed from a pale green at the edge through the various shades of blue to deepest blue and now as I looked over the edge of the reef from above, the deepest blue gave way to almost black at the edge of my vision. I swam out over the edge of the reef. The water was clear and I could see maybe 50 or 60 feet down before my vision revealed nothingness. I floated in the water above the reef nearly motionless and studied the sea beneath me through my face mask. I was mesmerized by the face of this reef. It looked like the face of a cliff.

The charts showed this reef running along the southern edge of this island varying in depth from a few inches to 50 or 60 feet and dropping away to several hundred feet. The only similar underwater configuration I could recall was the giant Mameroda rock at the entrance of Chub Cay in the Bahamas, where it rears up out of the sea on the very edge of the tongue of the ocean. They both must have been sheared away by some giant underwater disturbances eons in the past.

I wanted very much to go down and have a look, but about 30 feet is all I am capable of diving with only a snorkel. I had to content myself with floating above it in the clear water as I studied the reef face. I slowly kicked my way west along the edge of the deep water. After about 100 yards, the reef began to rise up gradually again until it was only about 20 feet below me before the east end dropped away to nothingness. Most of it was pristine and undisturbed, but I caught a glimpse of an object here and there with a symmetry that suggested human incursion at some time in the past.

The undersea life here was abundant. I could see dozens of nice sized fish. I saw a nurse shark about six foot long with its head poked beneath a rock, patiently working out a lobster dinner. I spotted several large Nassau Groupers with their dirty green stripes reflecting the light. I finally singled one out that was about 15 pounds. I took several deep breaths through my snorkel and kicked myself over, head down, toward the bottom. I came in on the grouper from a side angle and he seemed to watch me, unconcerned, out of his large liquid eye.

I approached to within 15 or 20 feet of him with my right arm extended and held the Sea Hornet spear gun like an extension of my arm. The fish still was unconcerned. It was so lazy it was almost a shame to spear it. Most undersea creatures show little fear of human divers as long as they don't make sudden or threatening moves, and my approach had been smooth and steady with only my power fins propelling me through the water.

I squeezed the trigger on the spear gun and the long thin stainless spear took the large grouper about four inches behind the gills. The fish made a feeble struggle and died. I tugged on the line that attached the spear to the barrel of the gun and brought the grouper to me. When I had my hand on the spear shank I gave a powerful kick to propel myself to the surface. I was about out of air. I broke the surface and blew hard with the last of the air in my lungs to clear the water from the barrel of my snorkel and gulped in the sweet fresh sea air.

I examined my catch. He was firmly pinioned on the spear shaft and held there by the spring at the point. It was much too large for my game bag, so I trailed the spear back along my side with the grouper still attached and kicked my way back in the direction of the rocky cay and my Avon. The giant power fins I favored made the return easy with little effort.

I was soon back by the Center Rock Cay where I had first entered the water. I swam to within a few feet of the rock still using only firm strokes with the power fins on my feet when the water shoaled up to about waist deep. I rolled over on my back and reached down with my free hand and slipped the heel strap of the fins off my diving boots one at a time and stood up in the warm Caribbean water. I surveyed the ocean and coast line and saw that we apparently still had this corner of the world all to ourselves.

I worked the big grouper off the spear head and carried it and my large diving fins ashore. I picked my way back across the small cay to where I had left the Avon about an hour earlier. It was still in place with its bow line tied to the shore shrub and its stern anchor line holding it off the rocky shore. I laid down the fish and inserted the spear back into the barrel of the gun, washed out the Avon, and pulled out the VHF radio, deciding to give Tobi a call. I switched the radio on and tuned to channel 18.

"Magic one to Magic." I repeated the call signs. I waited a few minutes and was about to press the send button again when Tobi answered loud and clear.

"Magic to Magic one, go ahead."

"Hi, Kid. Just thought I'd let you know we are having grilled grouper steaks for supper."

"Okay, great! I was sure we were having grilled fish. I already have the Hibachi set up on the rail. How was your dive?"

"Fine. Ill just slice off two large steaks form this fat grouper here on the cay and head back. and we can visit while supper's cooking. How's Peanut doing??

"He's still improving, I think. At least he's trying to be more active. But he sure is funny looking with his big head. Reminds me of a miniature buffalo, kinda."

"Well, don't let him be too active. I have work to do. See you soon. Magic One out."

I replaced the radio in its pouch and waded back ashore. I slipped my diving knife out of its calf sheath and laid the big grouper on a flat rock. I sliced in behind the gills, and, staying just above the rib bones, slid the knife down and out again just above the tail fin. I had one beautiful steak with not a bone in it. I flipped the fish over and repeated the process. In a couple of minutes I had my two steaks. I threw the remains back into the water, knowing the crabs and lobster would make a quick meal of them.

I untied the launch from shore and loaded up and pulled myself back to the stern anchor with the anchor rope. I soon had the small five-pound Danforth anchor aboard. I pulled the rope starter on the Yamaha engine and it roared to life on the first pull. I turned toward where Magic was anchored and twisted the throttle grip for more speed. I watched Magic becoming larger and larger as I closed the distance. She sure made a beautiful sight anchored in the harbor with the mountains of Roatan and the green jungle foliage in the background. No matter how many times I approached this yacht at anchor she always gave me a feeling of pride and well-being and security. It was enough that she was just there, so perfect and beautiful and belonging solely to me.

Tobi was up on deck watching my approach. I tossed her the bow line as I eased the launch alongside Magic.

"Come on aboard, Captain. I was starting to get lonesome."

"Can't afford to let that happen," I said as I stood up.

She made the line fast to a cleat and was reaching over the rail for the fish steaks and my diving gear. I handed everything up and climbed aboard. I gave her a kiss and said, "I missed you too."

"Sounds like the beginning of a subtle proposition to me, Captain," and gave me a saucy look.

"Could be, could be," I said, and patted her bottom gently.

"Want a drink?"

"Sounds good. You bartend. A rum and Coke for me. I think I will hook up the Avon and put it back on the davits."

"Being awfully cautious with the inflatable aren't you?"

"Well, probably. But since it's all we have left in way of a launch I damn well don't want anything to happen to it."

I pulled the Avon back to the stern and swung down off the stern rail to snap the two davit pulley ropes to the bow and stern of the launch and then swung myself back aboard. I pulled the hoist ropes and raised the Avon with motor attached up into place. I leaned over the davits and pulled the drain plug from the launch just in case it should rain.

When I turned back, Tobi was coming from below with a tray of drinks and some cheese-and-cracker snacks in her hand and her two escorts trailing at her heels. I was glad to see Peanut able to make the stairs under his own steam. She was right, he sure was funny looking. The swelling didn't seem to have gone down much. His head was still grotesque but his eyes seemed to have opened some. Tobi set the tray down on our round cocktail table in the center of the cockpit and I bent to fondle our two small companions. They were Tobi's dogs without a doubt. Just as Magic was my boat. But I shared her love for them and they always had a warm welcome for me. I examined and petted Peanut and made small talk to him until Coco decided enough was enough and pushed her way under my petting hand for her share of affection. I picked them both up and set them on the locker cushion and seated myself.

As soon as we were settled, Tobi said, "Well, how was your snorkel recon of the outside?"

I took her through the short trek I had from above the steep face of the reef and explained that I was very eager to have a look down below as soon as she was willing to come along.

"I think Peanut will be okay with Coco for a nurse tomorrow and we can take a scuba excursion off the reef. I don't want to be gone more than a couple of hours though. I'm sure he's going to be all right now, but I want to keep a close watch on him until he's back to normal."

"That's good. I want the sun to be well up so we'll have maximum light down below for our dive, and I want to be back up by two in the afternoon. That gives us almost an hour before the tide turns, and I don't want to be down below to test my theory on the suction created by its turning. I would just as soon as it stay theory for my part."

"Yes, me too."

"So, if we leave about eleven we can take two tanks each. That will give us about two hours each for our first look. That should be plenty of time for exploring and still have us back here by about two. And, by waiting until about eleven, the sun will be high enough for max light below.

"After I finish my drink I'll light the Hibachi and we can put the grouper on."

"Sounds good," she said. "Then maybe we can watch one of the new videos after dinner."

We had a pleasant meal. The grouper was delicious. We shared the cleanup chores, went below, and looked over the selection of video tapes we always keep aboard. After much discussion, we finally settled on *The Beverly Hills Cops*. We settled down in the pilot house and viewed the movie. It was light and funny and just the thing to finish out our fine evening. By nine, we were down below in our bunks with the tape deck sending out soft music.

Tobi said, "Jim, remember back home when we were talking about the old pirate cove and I was doing all the research on the old time ships that had disappeared in this area?"

"Yes, I remember. What about it?"

"Oh, I was just thinking how we had planned on coming here and then decided against it. After all the problems we had here in our first two ports on Roatan and the Peanut almost dying here. It's just kinda eerie, that's all. But I do want us to be very careful just in case we have been getting some kind of omen or warning or something. Oh, heck. I don't really know what I mean. I'm just not as enthused over this as I was back in the safety of La Dulce Vida. I'm just getting spooky. Oh, never mind. Forget I said anything. Goodnight, Baby Doll. See you in the morning. The sunshine always drives away my personal spooks."

"Goodnight, Tobi," I answered.

I lay in my bunk, turning over what she had said about omens and all and I was soon asleep.

I awoke with the sun slanting in the port side portal over my bunk, so it registered that we were still pointing bow out toward the sea. The boat hadn't moved during the night.

I threw my legs over the bunk to start my day, and Tobi said, "Morning, Handsome. I was just wondering if you were ever going to wake up."

Coco and Peanut were sitting up on Tobi's bunk wagging their good morning. "Well, Peanut, I see you're still with us." He gave a small bark in recognition of his name. He was still swelled up pretty good, but his head seemed some smaller to me.

Tobi said, "Peanut is lots better this morning. He and Coco have already been up on deck. He still looks awfully funny, but I don't think he even knows it now. I sure wish we knew what had happened to him. If we take them ashore again we need to know what to be on the lookout for. He was trying to get Coco to play on deck but it was too early for her. It's a beautiful day, no breeze hardly at all and the swells in the bay are down to almost nothing this morning."

"Good, then we'll finally get our chance for a look at the face of this reef. How are your spooks this morning?"

"All gone. Washed away by the sunshine I guess. I'm even good and ready to get started."

"Well, I still want the sun to be as high as possible, so how about we take a swim and then have a late breakfast. That way we can skip lunch or at least wait until we return from our dive."

"Sounds great to me. Is this swim suited or unsuited?"

"Well, you know I always did like you naked best."

"Ok, Captain. Naked it is."

CHAPTER 12

We stripped off the rest of our clothes, only cutoffs for me and short nightie for Tobi, and headed up the stairs for the deck naked as the day we were born. I released our boarding ladder from its fastener on the cabin top and slipped it into the stainless fasteners on the side of the hull. Without the ladder, it would be next to impossible to get aboard from the water except by climbing up the anchor chain, and that is not very easy.

Tobi dived over the rail and split the water clean. She is like poetry in motion in the water. Long, clean, smooth strokes. I never tired of watching her swim. I am a strong swimmer and much at home in the water, but smooth I am not. Peanut and Coco wanted to join the fun. Both were on their back legs with their front paws on the cap rail, studying Tobi closely.

"Come on in. Water's fine," she called.

"How about our small friends? They want to play too."

"I'll swim back and you can hand Coco down, but Peanut has to stay aboard for a few days."

I picked Coco up and leaned far over. Tobi swam under me to catch Coco. Coco is an excellent swimmer but doesn't like her eyes to get sea water in them. So Tobi caught her and let her down easy. I admonished Peanut to stay put and dove over the rail to join my family.

We swam and played for half an hour. I swam around Magic and gave her hull a close up inspection. I tried to go down and check the anchors but ran out of air with still five or six feet to go to the bottom. I was really just playing as I knew we were down good and solid after the blow. A strong pull on our anchor just makes it dig down deeper, so I was sure we were down good and deep.

Tobi called out, "Coco and I are going to get out. I'll start breakfast."

"Good enough. I'm coming out too."

Once aboard, we toweled off and got dressed in shorts and T-shirts. Tobi headed for the galley, and I returned topside and started laying out our diving gear. I placed our diving bags on the deck and began putting tanks, buoyancy vests, fins, knives, and the like in the bags.

Tobi almost always wore a wet suit, but she kept that in her closet below. She had been lobster diving with me several years ago off Gun Cay in the Bahamas in only a skimpy bikini and we were looking under a ledge for dinner when she somehow got her leg against a head of fire coral. It was not a problem for a day or so, but then she went from a skin rash to real sores on her leg. She carried the marks of this encounter for several months. Now she almost always dons wet suits and gloves before a dive in salt water.

I finally had our gear sorted out with an extra tank apiece, which would give us about two hours each in the water if we didn't exert ourselves and burn up our supply extra fast. Tobi was calling me from below that breakfast was on, so I zipped up our diving bags and headed below for breakfast, eager to get started.

After breakfast, we cleaned up and played with the dogs. Peanut was feeling fine. He still had a big head, but he didn't seem to mind it very much. About ten-thirty, I let our Avon down into the water and maneuvered it alongside Magic. Tobi started handing down our diving gear from the deck. The air bottles and weighted belts were pretty heavy for her but she insisted on doing her share, so I stayed in the Avon and stored the gear as she handed it over. As usual, she was up to the task, and I had learned it was better not to argue with her when she set out to do something. She put the dogs below and secured the screen door so they couldn't come up on deck and get into mischief while we were away. This completed, she climbed over the rail and down into the Avon with me.

Tobi was smiling from ear to ear with eagerness for our new adventure. She was looking good in her skin-tight black wet suit with pink and green fluorescent stripes in contrast with my cutoff jeans and diving boots. We retraced my route of the day before, and I decided to leave the launch in the same place on the inside in sheltered water. It would take only a few minutes for me to carry our gear across the rock, and once in the water the weights and tanks would be no problem.

We eased the launch up to the sheltered side of the rock again, and I slipped over the side in waist-deep water and took a line ashore. Tobi stayed in the Avon and helped me drag our bags over the side where we set them ashore. She slipped over the side and I threw out the small stern anchor. I took the two heavy bags and gave her the spear guns, and we covered the few paces to the ocean side of the rock. We donned our weights and gloves and carried our fins and pushed the tanks attached to our buoyancy vests into the water where we could slip into them with less trouble than on shore. It was a few minutes before eleven by this time, and we turned on our air supply and cleared our regulators. I led off and kicked myself toward the deeper water at the edge of the reef.

We had a beautiful day for our sport. The day was clear and the sunshine very bright. The sun was almost overhead. The sea swells were moderate and the water visibility was superb. When we came near the edge of the cliff, I motioned for Tobi to catch up with me. I spit out my regulator mouth cup and said, "I want you to stay with me. Don't go wandering off on your own today."

"Okay." She nodded her agreement and smiled and gave me a thumbs up and then pointed down. I cleared my regulator again and put my head down and started slowly for the edge of the underwater cliff. We paused around 35 feet down for a few minutes to let our ears and bodies adjust to the change in pressure and then continued over the edge of the cliff.

The face here was sheer and looked like a canyon. Marine life abounded, and as we went deeper the fish got larger, the larger fish preferring the deeper and cooler water. The visibility was still excellent. I could see the bottom of the cliff face now. It was only about

30 to 35 feet from top to bottom here, then the bottom shelved out almost flat again. The shelf was covered with rocks of different sizes and a lot of sand over the shelf in places. I swam over the shelf, holding about 10 feet above the bottom, still heading south or toward the open sea.

After about 150 feet, the shelf ended abruptly. This cliff face was much like the first one, only I got the impression it was much larger. I had been swimming over a plateau, or wide ledge, in this under sea canyon where nature or some force had sheared this ledge off, so flat I was again going down a sheer cliff face into the unknown at greater depths.

I continued on down to 140 feet, and the visibility was down a few feet and the water was getting colder. I motioned to Tobi and we started our ascent. We were not going to go any deeper down the face of this second cliff. Nothing to see this deep and we couldn't stay long even if there were.

We returned to the flat shelf between the first and second cliff, and I swam back towards shore for 50 feet or so, still holding 10 or 12 feet above the bottom. I had a good view of the bottom and could see the face of the first cliff. I turned east and kicked myself over the bottom with a smooth, steady pace.

Before we had traveled far, I saw a coral encrusted anchor. It looked like a rock but in the shape of an anchor of the type used by the old Windjammers of two or three hundred years ago. It would have weighed several hundred pounds. I studied it from my position above and Tobi brushed against me and pointed down at it. She had spotted it also. I nodded and we went down to have a closer look.

We could find nothing else that looked as if it came from a ship. Once we were close enough to touch it, it didn't even look like an anchor any longer, just a large rock. But I knew it was definitely an anchor that had been in the ocean for a long time, letting the coral form around it, still holding its shape but losing its identity in the rock covering process. There was no evidence of chain or anything else that I could see. If there had been other debris from a ship here the sea had long ago claimed it. I shrugged to Tobi and we took up our former positions over the bottom and swam on eastward.

In another 50 yards or so I saw another rough shape of yet another ancient anchor. I motioned to Tobi and she nodded her agreement. We went down for a closer look. It was much the same as the first one. We looked the bottom over carefully but if there had been anything there the sand and small rocks had long ago hidden it from view.

Again we decided to continue on eastward, but as I started to proceed I noticed changes in the cliff surface. Nothing I could identify from here, but somehow different. Large dark spots were fading in and out of my vision. My subconscious mind was telling me that these were caused by deeper indents or cavities, or possibly small caves. I turned north to bring us in closer to the cliff. As we neared the rock face I could see changes in the sheer wall; it was becoming more craggy, and the dark spots that had caught my eye turned out to be small holes and craters in the rock face. These seemed to vary in size from a few inches across to a few feet. The face was honeycombed with them. As we came up to the cliff face, we could see that most went in only a foot or so while others seemed to go much deeper.

We worked our way slowly along the rocky face until we were only about five feet away from the rocky, perpendicular surface. Suddenly, Tobi grabbed at my leg from her position at my side and just slightly behind me. I glanced at her to see what she wanted, and she was pointing to the rocky surface just a few feet above my head. I stared in the direction she was indicating and finally saw what had riveted her attention.

Only a few feet above my head was one of the largest moray eels that I had ever seen. He was backed into one of the holes in the cliff face with only his ugly head protruding. His head was larger than both my fists combined. His mottled, sickly skin and small beady eyes were enough to make chills run up and down my spine. He was just sitting in his hole and staring directly at me. He wasn't doing anything aggressive, but he didn't need to. I back peddled slowly, Tobi following my lead, not taking our eyes off him and he watched us just as intently. We kept this up until I had put enough distance between us that he faded from vision and blended into the craggy face of the cliff.

I signaled my thanks to Tobi as we continued our way along the cliff face, staying a little farther away from its rocky face now. A short distance farther, the bottom began to change with the rocks lying on the bottom growing larger and scattered patches of live coral surrounded with sea fans waving their bright colors at us from their place on the ocean bottom. The change in the face of the cliff was evident, the dark patches growing larger and darker. We angled in closer to the cliff face. Now I could see several sure-enough caves in the rocky face. I swam toward one that appeared very large.

The cave mouth started about four feet up the cliff face from the rocky bottom. The cave appeared to be about 10 feet high and about the same in width. The water in the cave was of a much darker blue than the water around the outside of the cave. As I came up to the mouth of the cave, I noticed that the water in front seemed to drop a few degrees. I swam into the cave opening a short distance. The visibility dropped to about two feet. With so little light from above entering the cave it suddenly became very dark, so there was very little of the cave that my sight revealed, but my other senses told me this cave was large. My mind was automatically computing water temperature, visibility, feeling of space, and many things that past experience triggered. I had a feeling it could be growing larger.

I knew if we were to look any farther in the cave I would need our powerful underwater lights. Also, our air was down to about 15 minutes. I hadn't pulled the J-valve reserve as yet but knew the tank was getting close to empty. Keeping a close eye on the reserves could mean the difference between life and death for a diver.

I motioned to Tobi, who was right by my side. I tapped my Seiko dive watch and pointed up toward the surface, indicating that it was time we start up. She nodded her agreement and we backed out of the cave opening. We went back up to the top of the sheer face and took a short breather. My air was getting pretty hard to pull through my regulator, so I reached back to the bottom of my tank and pulled the rod down to give me the reserve air in the tank. I saw Tobi do likewise. We tarried a few more minutes in about 20 feet of water and then began to rise the short way to the surface.

When we broke the surface, we were about 50 feet or so east of the break in the reef that formed the channel leading into Port Royal. The water shoaled up fast here, hitting the reef that was only about three feet below the surface a short distance from us. I spit out my regulator mouth piece and pulled the mouth piece on my floater vest free of its Velcro fastener and blew a few short breaths of air into it in order to support the weight of the now nearly empty scuba tank. This accomplished, I yelled at Tobi, "Well, Kid, what do you think of Fowler Reef now?"

CHAPTER 13

Tobi shook out her wet hair and replied. "Fowler Reef isn't so bad so far, but we didn't get to do much exploring yet. I'd like to see where the cave goes, at least for a short distance. How about you?"

"Yeah, me too. But we need our power lights and some line. We don't want to put ourselves in danger. Let's head back to the rock where our launch is."

We pulled over our snorkels from the side of our diving masks where they were fixed with a rubber keeper and turned back west toward where we had entered the ocean. Once back on the rock we sat down side by side and relaxed in the bright sun for a few minutes.

"Well, Tobi, we still have another tank. What do you say?"

"I say let's save it for tomorrow. I'm a little pooped and want to get back to Magic and check on the babies."

"Okay by me. We'll give it a better look tomorrow."

We started gathering up our gear and were soon putting back toward our yacht in the rubber Avon. Back aboard, the dogs were glad to see us and voiced their greeting. Tobi went below to scare up some lunch, and I got out the hose and connected it to the fresh water pump and began washing the salt from our diving gear. This chore completed, I set out the Bauer air compressor and started its gasoline engine. I hooked up one of our empty tanks and began refilling it. It takes about 20 minutes to pump 3000 pounds of air into a scuba tank with this Bauer Nova compressor, but it's so portable you can use it anywhere and it's well worth the $3500 I paid for it in Miami a couple of years before. It has a safety pop-off valve that will pop off when the tank has 3200 psi, so I don't have to watch the pressure gauge continuously.

I moved about the deck, repacking our bags for another planned dive the next day. The weather was perfect and the harbor was peaceful, the quiet broken only by the engine of the air compressor laboring at its task. I got back to the compressor and the gauge showed a little more than 3100 pounds, so I closed the tank valve and unscrewed the first tank and hooked up the second tank and opened its valve to let it begin filling. Just as I straightened up, Tobi came back up the deck with a large glass of iced tea in hand and her two dogs at her heels.

She said, "I thought the captain might be thirsty."

"I am, but was so busy I hadn't noticed." I took the tea and downed about half.

"Lunch is about ready. How long before you can kill that noisy thing?"

"Almost finished. Another 15 minutes and we are full of air again and ready for tomorrow."

"Good. I'll start setting lunch on deck under the awning."

I soon had the second bottle filled and killed the compressor. I decided to let it cool down before storing it in the deck locker, so I headed aft to a well-deserved lunch.

After lunch, we decided to take the dogs ashore so they could run and play. We agreed to only go to the beach today. Since we weren't sure what had bitten Peanut—or where—the beach seemed like a safe bet. Peanut seemed to agree with our decision as he seemed a bit skittish about a return trip to shore.

We lazed in the afternoon sunshine at the edge of the water on the fine white sand and watched our two four-legged friends get their exercise chasing the small pale ghost crabs that inhabited this area. We made small talk for a while in the peace and quiet of the beach with only the sound of the water running a short way up the sand and then running swiftly back to join the water of the bay. After about an hour the dogs had spent their excess energy and came back to lie in the sand close to Tobi and watch her as if to say, "Okay, now what next?"

She said, "Well, the puppies have had enough exercise and I think I might like to trade this sand for my bunk and a book. How about you, Captain?"

"Sounds good to me. I'll do a few chores and maybe have a nap."

We loaded up and were back aboard Magic in a few minutes. I decided to pull the Avon up on the davits again. Still nervous about the whaler, I guess. Tobi and her charges disappeared below and I was left alone on deck with my chores. I hooked the snaps to the Avon and pulled it up in place and cleated the restraining ropes, then I went forward and put the now cool air compressor in the storage box.

I repacked our diving bags and then set our two battery powered mobile diving lights out on deck. I unclipped the stainless steel fasteners from the bright yellow plastic water proof housing. I checked the watertight seals and they looked fine, so I hooked the battery terminals to the powerful marine battery and closed the inspection plates. I pressed the handle trigger and the large light flared to life. I pressed the second trigger switch and the small plastic propeller also started. Satisfied with the results, I repeated the procedure on the second light.

Finally, when I could think of nothing more needing attention, I went below. Tobi and her two charges were in her starboard bunk. Her puppies were watching me quietly from beneath hooded eyes and Tobi with a book open and lying on her chest was fast asleep with a smile on her face. I wondered what thoughts or dreams were chasing through her unconscious mind to bring a smile to the surface. I lay down quietly on my bunk so as not to disturb her and began to go over the day's events and our preliminary dive on the Fowler Reef. I was soon asleep.

Coming back to life from my place in the sleep world, I heard a soft humming or some such pleasant sound, and, easing my eyes open, I was rewarded with the sight of Tobi standing there.

"Hey, Big Boy, you want something to eat or are you on a fast?"

I sat up and looked around. It was early twilight. I glowered at my watch. It was 10 past eight. "Wow, I must have been tired, I was only going to rest for a few minutes."

"Yes, I know. Same for me. I've only been up for a few minutes. I was full of pee or I probably would still be asleep myself. How about a light supper, maybe sandwiches and iced tea?"

"Sounds good to me. I'm not really all that hungry."

She headed back to the galley and I went up on deck to take a leak over the side and just look around. It was still peaceful, the harbor smooth as glass. Hardly a breeze. Magic lay dead in the water, not moving, her anchor chain slack. I could hear the howler monkeys on shore fussing about some unseen intruder. It was a beautiful evening. I love the quiet. I savored the solitude and privacy that only a boat at anchor in a little known wilderness harbor can offer.

#

What the captain of Magic could not know was that the privacy and isolation he was feeling at that moment were only an illusion. Two men were sitting in a concealed nest they had arranged in the hillside high above the harbor. Hidden from view from below, they watched every move the man on the black yacht made. Speaking to each other in low, muted voices that would not carry more than a few feet in the bushy, vegetated area, they were intent on what they were doing.

Carlos said to his companion, "I hate that dude. I don't like the way he walk, the way he talk, the way he look. He think he so high and mighty. But he won't be so proud in a little bit. I gonna fuck him up real good. I gonna fuck his white whore and make her scream and bleed. I gonna eat her damn dogs, though they won't hardly make a meal."

Zep cut him off in the same hushed voice. "Easy, Carlos. All things come to those who wait, if they have patience and planning, and are smart, like we is. What them stupid people don't know is that that boat, their money, the dive stuff—everything—belongs to us. We just let them use it a little bit longer. We just need to know what they is looking for, or if they find something here. 'Cause what they find, it belong to us too."

#

I went back inside and could hear Tobi humming to herself in the galley while she busied herself making our supper. After supper we shared scullery duty. I washed and she dried the dishes. Cleaning chores done Tobi said, "You feel like getting beat up at gin?"

"Well, I would like a good game but finding a worthy opponent way out here will be a problem."

"Huh! You said too much already. You're on."

We played gin until around midnight and the score pad clearly showed she had made good her bragging and beat me up real bad.

"Well, Kid, I think I could take another nap. How about you?"

"I'll get out my book. It's sure to put me to sleep. It nearly always does. Same schedule for tomorrow?"

"Yes, I think so. Late breakfast. Take the dogs ashore awhile, and dive around midday again tomorrow."

CHAPTER 14

I woke early, the sun slanting in through the port side portals again. I glanced at my watch. It was just past seven in the morning. I was full of energy and eager to start the day. I looked over at Tobi. She was still asleep but both her dogs were watching me carefully. I eased myself into an upright position and slipped on my cut-offs and headed up on deck. Both dogs decided to come along. I went up on deck and made for the side rigging to take my morning leak over the side. The dogs headed forward to do the same. I went back to the stern davits and began to uncleat the Avon, deciding to let it down early.

I heard Tobi calling from below. "Hey, you guys all jump ship? Or just mad cause I beat you so bad at gin?"

"No, we're just full of energy today and don't want to spend such a beautiful day in bed."

"Give me a sec and I'll join you." I heard her close the door to the head below.

I sat down on the side bench seat in the cockpit near the large varnished wooden wheel with its brass bolts and fittings. I was admiring the boat as I have done hundreds of time when both dogs came charging down the deck from the bow to join me. They settled down, one on either side of me vying for attention. They preferred the company of Tobi but would settle for me when she wasn't around. I stretched out a hand to each of them and began to stoke each in turn. Peanut's head was about back to normal size now and he displayed little or no evidence of his near fatal ordeal. They were both of a calm disposition and my heart went out to both of them.

I spotted Tobi coming up the steps to join us. She looked beautiful that morning, her long thick blonde tresses brushed to a brilliant sheen and tied back with a pink ribbon. Her long tanned, well-formed legs poked out of a pair of skin tight white shorts topped with a black T-shirt displaying a ship's wheel with an anchor in the center in gold with "Magic" written in the same gold color just above the emblem. The T-shirt looked beautiful on her and she filled the front out to perfection.

She said. "Good morning, guys. Thought you had all abandoned the ship when I awoke with no one around."

"No, we just awoke early and were eager to be up and about. Say, how come the Magic shirts always look so much better on you than me?"

"Girl's secret," she said. "But you don't look bad in them yourself, Captain. So, what's up? Breakfast, or what?"

I glanced at the dogs and we all looked back at Tobi. "Well, I think breakfast will be fine and then we can take the puppies back ashore for a while and while they expend their excess energy we can lie around on the beach and conserve ours for our mid-day excursion."

"Sounds like a good plan to me. She gave me a kiss and said, "Don't know if I told you lately, but I sure do love you. You just relax and I'll fix up something."

She disappeared below and her dogs followed, leaving me alone on deck. I leaned back on my bench seat and began to visualize this harbor filled with ships. What must it have been like a few hundred years ago? I could almost wish I had lived back then, to experience the rough, exciting life of seafaring people back then. They had to be a very special and hardy breed. Cruel I am sure. But life itself was cruel in those times.

The heyday of the pirate in the Western world lasted less than 20 years. In those few years they created enough havoc with their cruel, destructive, yet carefree ways that the stories would probably go on forever. Today, the pirates we hear about are not very colorful or romantic. They're just common thieves that chance has placed near water and the opportunity to prey on the unwary traveler with a yacht. I've had a few chance meetings with that sort, such as right here in the Bay Islands. But I don't think any real danger exists today to compare with the pirate of days gone by.

I'm not sure how long I was wool gathering but Tobi was calling up from the galley. "Hey, Big Guy, come in before your pancakes get cold."

I came out of my reverie and stood and stretched and headed below. There is a square door about one foot high and 18 inches long set behind the pilot house dinette so that food or refreshments can be passed directly up from the galley to the pilot house when the door is open. Tobi was just below this serving door now. I went over and peered down at her. She had a large plate of pancakes ready to pass up to me. She passed up the pancakes, link sausages, jam, white Karo syrup that I prefer, and a large pitcher of iced milk made from powder. I set things out on the table and Tobi came up the steps to join me. We had a quiet breakfast. As usual we shared the cleaning chores. This finished, we loaded the Avon I had pulled alongside earlier and headed for the beach.

I jumped out and pulled the launch up on the white sand and Peanut and Coco bounded out and were off up the beach in pursuit of whatever excitement they could find. I gave Tobi my hand and she stepped ashore carrying two large beach towels saying "Thank you" in her playful voice. She spread the large towels side by side and settled down on one, patting the other for me to join her. I glanced at the launch to make sure it was high enough on the beach that it wouldn't float off. Satisfied it was safe, I plopped down on the other towel beside Tobi.

She said, "What do you think of those two large anchors we saw? How do you think they came to be there?"

"Well, of course I don't know, but there are many possibilities."

"I realized that you can't know for sure," she said, "but I just love it when you make up stories about what you think happened. You always make it seem so real."

"Well, okay, what could have happened is perhaps two large pirate ships, either together or at different times, were making for Port Royal. Perhaps they had damage to the rudder, or the rigging, maybe after a sea battle, or a fierce storm. Anyway, for some reason they weren't able to negotiate the channel into the inner harbor. So, when they were in water that was shallow enough for them to drop their giant anchors, they did so, trying to hold off the rocky shore. Maybe until the sea went down or until they could make repairs and gain the safety of Port Royal.

"They may even have been captured prizes that couldn't have been brought into port for the same reason. However, for some reason, nature or God knows what, I don't believe they ever made the harbor. I believe the ships were smashed to pieces against the reef there on each side of the channel, leaving only the two great anchors as evidence that some event had taken place here."

"What do you think happened to the people on board?"

"There's no way of telling. I would guess they most probably perished. It would be close to a miracle if you got a ship on that reef in bad weather and were able to swim ashore. It's possible that a few of the tough and hearty seamen could have made it, but I don't believe many would have been that lucky."

"It must have been terrible to live in those times. I'm so glad we live in civilized times."

"If you say so. But look at all the valuable stuff they had with them. Nice souvenirs left behind for anyone lucky enough to find them."

"Looks like there would be lots more stuff below, doesn't it?"

"Oh, I'm sure there was at the time. However, you know how the sea has its own way of cleaning itself with time. It's even hidden the anchors themselves in a rock covering so that only an experienced eye could ever detect them. No, the other debris has long since been swept out to sea or over the cliff edge, or been covered with sand or marine growth of some sort. The sea has just hid whatever evidence there was of these ships passing in its own way."

I looked back at Tobi and then out at Magic sitting at anchor and looking so majestic in the picturesque setting of old Port Royal, and for the thousandth time I thought how fortunate I had been in life. Almost like a dream come true.

Tobi broke in and said, "A penny for your thoughts?"

"Oh, just reminiscing about how lucky we've been. Getting to live some of our dreams when others just as worthy never do."

"Yes, I know exactly what you mean. I pinch myself sometimes just to make sure I'm not dreaming. I've traveled far for an orphan girl child born in Tulsa, Oklahoma. God, I'm grateful that we found each other." She leaned over and put her arms around me and kissed me deeply.

The dogs saw our embrace and darted back to our towels so as not to be excluded from this obvious display of affection. We laughed together and the spell was broken. We embraced our small dogs.

The dogs seemed to have had their fill of exercise for the morning, so by mutual agreement we began gathering up our towels and pets to return to the boat. Coco and Peanut bounded into the launch, eager to be back aboard Magic. Tobi climbed in and I shoved the Avon back into the waters of the bay and leaped aboard myself. I settled into the stern, gave the Yamaha engine pull rope a swift pull, and the little engine purred to life. I pointed it toward Magic and soon had us alongside the sleek black hull.

Tobi handed the dogs up to deck level and scampered up the ladder herself, giving me a pleasing view of a perfectly formed and tantalizing backside. I thought to myself that if I wasn't very careful we would be late for our planned dive on Fowler Reef.

I climbed aboard and tied the launch off. Tobi fixed us a Coke with ice, and we relaxed on the aft deck in the shade of our large black canvas sun awning for a few minutes before loading our dive gear into the launch. Tobi put her small dogs inside the hatch and admonished them to be good, that we would be back soon. She closed the screen door and secured it. I went forward for our dive bags and gear and began carrying them back just past midship on the starboard side where we could hand it down into the launch.

We had quite a stack of gear now that we had added the large power diving lights to our store of other necessities. We had decided to leave the spear guns behind this trip. The power lights required both hands for efficient maneuverability under water. And it wasn't like there was any danger we'd have to protect against. I climbed down into the rubber launch and Tobi handed down the gear. We were soon headed for the rocky cay in the harbor center, retracing our route of the day before.

Once again we crossed the rocky cay after securing our launch and began laying out our gear. We secured the diving light to our inflatable vests by means of a thick nylon cord about five feet long so they wouldn't float off if we turned loose of the grips.

These lights are equipped with small guide planes at the housing front so that the diver can move the hand grips and guide the powered light up or down. This control is achieved by merely by pulling the trigger that controls the plastic propeller at the stern and twisting the hands in the desired direction.

We stepped into the warm water of the Caribbean with the bright sun high in the sky and slipped into our vest and fins. I cautioned Tobi to stay close by me, especially in the cave, and we agreed to use only one light if the beam was sufficient for us both to explore. We turned on our air tanks and cleared our regulators. We pulled our masks in place, and I put my head down and headed for the bottom with Tobi close behind me. I pulled the trigger on the power light, engaging only the propeller. This would save the light until it was needed.

We stopped at a rock shaped like a crude arrowhead just at the edge of the first cliff for a few moments to let our bodies adjust to being underwater. I looked at Tobi and she nodded her head that she was ready. I went over the edge of the cliff head down and again leveled off about 10 feet above the plateau at the base of the first cliff. I turned east, paralleling the rocky face once again. I had the power light out in front of me at arm's length, letting it pull me smoothly through the water. I gave small flicks of my ankles so the large power fins on my feet would help me along.

Tobi was on my left side only slightly behind me. I glanced sideways at her stroking smoothly through the deep, looking like some beautiful psychedelic sea creature. We soon saw the first rock-encrusted anchor below us. Shortly after, the second came into view. We were making good progress. I saw the rocky face of the cliff changing as we continued on eastward. Soon we were in front of the cave we had selected the day before.

I stopped for a moment and looked at Tobi. She hit the light trigger on her power light and it flared brilliantly to life, slicing through the water like a giant laser knife. I did likewise, just to assure myself that the light was working still. We cut the light after a brief test as they weren't needed at this depth where the sunlight could still penetrate the water. She looked at me and gave a thumbs up and pointed to the cave entrance. I nodded my agreement and turned toward the cave mouth. The cave was more like a tunnel, about 10 feet high and 10 feet wide at the entrance. The floor of the tunnel was flat, for the most part, with the top and sides giving the impression of being oval shaped.

We entered easily side by side. After penetrating the tunnel only a few feet, I noticed the water was several degrees cooler. The visibility abruptly dropped to zero, like something had cast us blind. I pulled the trigger on my powerful light and it penetrated the dark depth like a knife. I glanced at my watch and wrist compass in the light's afterglow. It was 11:20 in the morning, and we were now headed north, back toward the Island of Roatan or maybe under the island itself. I moved the light about gently to examine what lay ahead. It still appeared to be only a cave or tunnel under the sea.

The cave floor appeared to have been swept clean by some giant sea creature; there were no small stones or sand or sea debris of any kind on the floor of this tunnel. It was strange for me. I had never seen any underwater area as clean or sterile looking as this place. Tobi was very close beside me now, and I suspected she was feeling some of the same uneasiness I was experiencing. I inched forward a few more feet and could see that the cave was widening out a short distance ahead. I couldn't tell much about it from this vantage point, but could see—and sense—some change.

We moved slowly forward, watching our surroundings in the beam of the light. It felt like we had been placed on some strange alien planet, and in a sense we had. Soon it was obvious that the cave had widened out into a large room. As we floated in the entrance and slowly moved the beam around, we observed the cave room was about 30 feet across and the walls were more craggy, not worn and smooth as they had been in the tunnel leading there. The floor seemed to slope downward very gradually. It also had changed and there were large rocks in various shapes scattered along the floor. Tobi was still very close on my left side and showed no inclination to put any distance between us or to go wandering off on her own just then. I went another 40 or 50 feet into the room and then the light was reflecting back off the wall at the far end, so apparently the cave finished there.

I felt a surge of disappointment. I was hoping it would not disprove my theory so early about the blue holes of the Bahama Bank maybe connecting with this part of the Caribbean. But obviously this cave came to an end here and could not be connected anywhere.

I continued on toward the wall marking the end of the cave. The light revealed that this end wall was pockmarked with small crater-like holes similar to those on the outside face of the cliff, evidence of the constant action of the sea over time. Also, along the end wall were piles of stones and sand varying in size from a few inches to a few feet. When I was only 12 or 14 feet from the curve marking the end of the cave, my light showed an area to my right that had been hidden from my view previously. I experienced a thrill and uplifting of spirits. This wasn't the end of this cave after all! It only made a sharp right turn and narrowed back to its former size of 10 to 12 feet in height and width.

While I was experiencing this and just about to continue into this tunnel, I was conscious of Tobi activating her light. She had it aimed directly at the back wall of the cave room. She moved toward one of the pocket-like craters about a foot wide and 18 inches high. She motioned frantically for me to come closer to where she was. I could sense her urgency, so I moved quickly toward her position and shined my light into the pocket she was indicating. She cut her light and turned it loose, allowing it to float free on the line attached to her vest. She began digging in the pocket with her gloved hands and soon held up a piece of bright metal about the size of a silver dollar. It was obviously solid gold.

#

Carlos and his friend were still watching the black yacht from their secluded place on the thick, bushy hillside above the harbor of Port Royal. They had observed the Americans loading the small rubber launch with bags and what looked to be diving gear.

Zep said, "You know, Carlos, we find a few gold coins off that reef and we barter a few more from them lobster divers before they start going missing, and they what was left got spooked and wouldn't dive there no more. And you know we make more off the few coins we got than we ever did off anything we do ever before. And that guy on the mainland who buy them ask lots of questions and want more coins plenty bad. So we know they worth plenty. We just never could figure out where they come from, just scattered about, one here, one someplace else. We just ain't figured it out yet.

Now maybe we won't have to. I think that stupid bastard on the black boat plenty smart. I think he work for us and figure it all out for us, so he make us very rich, important men. I think he find the rest of our treasure for us. And you be sure it is our treasure and he and his woman work themselves to death for us on our treasure.

CHAPTER 15

I stared incredulously at the piece of metal Tobi held in her gloved hand. Only gold holds its former brilliance in sea water and resists all marine growth. I could feel her excitement and I was feeling such a rush of adrenaline that I wanted to drop my light and join her at the crater. But I disciplined myself to hold fast and stretched out my hand for her to hand me the gold disk. It was a large gold coin. I couldn't tell much else about it in this environment, but I was sure that it was very old. Tobi broke in on my contemplation by waving her hand excitably in front of the light beam and proudly displaying another coin. She slipped this one into her vest pocket and smoothed the Velcro fasteners, securing the pocket, and returned to the crater in the cave face like a gopher to its hole.

I watched her, mesmerized, as she sorted through the debris in the hole. After a few minutes of this, she glanced back at me and indicated another pocket just to her left and about two feet farther up the wall, just at the edge of our light pattern. I looked at my watch and gave her a negative shake of the head. We had been down about 40 minutes so far and I wanted to give us plenty of time to get out of the cave and back to the surface. We needed to spend about 10 minutes around the 30-foot level on our ascent for safety's sake. We weren't really working deep enough for pressure to be a real problem, but I wanted to play it safe. Tobi gave me a reluctant shrug and pulled her light back to her by its retaining cord. I signaled for her to lead off and I would follow her out and back to the surface.

We retraced our way back out of the cave to open water at the cliff face and headed up. We stopped at 30 feet for a few minutes and I could tell she was bursting with excitement and impatient to return to the surface to discuss her find. In all our years of diving, this was the first time we had found any gold. After a few minutes she pointed up. I nodded my head in agreement and we made for the surface.

We broke the surface again on the east side of the channel and Tobi spit out her mouth piece and yelled, "Whoopee! Whoopee!" She tried to give me a hug but was not quite able to pull it off with both our buoyancy vests in between.

She said, "Let's get our spare air. I want to get back to my cave."

We headed back to our rock for the spare bottles. I was eager as Tobi to get back down there. When we made the rocky cay I decided to retrieve the Avon this time and take it to the outside where we had surfaced earlier. The sea was so smooth now that I could anchor the launch in shallow water well out from the rocky reef where it broke the water with little fear of damage. With the sea this calm, we would have little trouble diving from the Avon. We gathered up all our things and stored them in the Avon, then headed around the cay for the channel leading out of Port Royal Harbor towards the open sea.

Tobi was a sight to see. She was all smiles and looked like she had just won the ten million dollar lottery, and it dawned on me that maybe she had.

We took the Avon through the channel and turned left, going to a spot near where we had surfaced a short while before. The water there was only about five feet deep and shoaled up fast to expose the rocky reef. I kept the launch out far enough that I didn't think the swells could carry it onto the rocks. Here I threw out our small five-pound anchor and reminded myself to be sure and check that it was in good holding when I went over the side.

Tobi and I busied ourselves changing our air tanks and preparing ourselves for another hour in our underwater cave. We were soon finished and ready to get underway again.

She said, "I've got about a million things to tell you and a million more questions to ask, but will have to save them for tonight. I'm too excited to talk right now anyway."

I smiled and said, "Likewise. But let's don't get careless in our excitement. This is what we have been dreaming about for years and I want it to have a happy ending."

"No sweat, Captain. Let's go."

We sat on the inflated rubber edge of the launch facing in and just fell over backwards into the Caribbean. Once in the water I looked around the bottom for our small Danforth anchor and saw it firmly hooked under the edge of a small coral head. This satisfied me that the launch wouldn't go anywhere in our absence. I looked around at Tobi and she signaled for me to lead us back down. I started for the edge of the cliff and pointed my high-powered light straight down.

In minutes, we were back over our underwater plateau and only a few yards from the cave mouth. As we headed for the entrance, we paused only a moment to look at one another and reentered the cave side by side. I turned on the power to my light once again and headed to the rear of the cave room.

It dawned on me again that maybe my theory of these caves connecting with the blue holes on the banks wasn't so far-fetched after all. At least this cave didn't end here and it had turned in the general direction of the bank when it turned back northeast. I cautioned myself to pay attention and think of these things later.

We were back at the rocky face again where Tobi had found her cache of coins earlier. She pointed to another crater up slightly higher on the wall. I signaled her to go ahead and positioned the light to her best advantage. She allowed her light to float free on its retaining cord and peered into the other pocket. I couldn't see much of what she was doing, but she was in her gopher position again clinging to the rock face and digging in the sand and debris that was trapped in the pocket.

After only a few minutes she turned toward me and flashed yet another coin in my direction before squirreling it away in her vest and returning to her digging. We went from crater to crater in this manner, digging and searching each pocket or crater within reach that caught her eye, all located at the cave's end where it took a sharp right turn and narrowed again. I held the light and Tobi did all the searching and directing from one hole to another. It seemed only minutes since we had returned, but my watch said differently. It was now a few minutes past one, and we were going to have to start for the surface again.

I signaled Tobi to shut down her digging and catch up her light. I wanted to have a quick look down the tunnel before leaving. Tobi back by my side, I turned my light around and headed for the tunnel leading off the room. We entered cautiously and saw it was similar to the cave entrance. We swam only 40 feet or so along this tunnel and realized it was going deeper. I glanced at the depth gauge fastened to my vest and noted that we had descended another 15 feet in depth while progressing northeast for another 40 feet.

Satisfied that this tunnel went somewhere and showed no signs of ending, I signaled Tobi we had gone far enough. Here again there was no sand or debris in this tunnel. It was swept clean. All the sand and pebbles were trapped in the crater and face of the cave room. We had enough room to turn around, so we worked our way back to the large underwater room.

Just as we entered the next room, my light picked up two bright red sapphire points of light and a big dark shape. My heart skipped a beat and I threw out my left hand for Tobi not to pass me. I studied the dark shape and sapphire eyes very carefully and eased my way forward very slowly. I knew that there was a sea creature of impressive proportions between us and open water, and we didn't even have a spear gun. I had a large, stainless steel diving knife, razor sharp, strapped to my right thigh, but I knew it would be nearly useless against this brute.

I eased a few more feet toward this monster and it stared straight at the light as if hypnotized. We had to get out of there soon or we were going to have to sprout gills. Our air bottles were getting near the critical stage. With no other choice, I kept going slowly toward this monster, hoping against hope that we would be able to swim by it and knowing damn well we wouldn't be able to.

Then the monster began to take shape. It was about 12 to 14 feet long. Judging by the torpedo shape and smooth graceful lines, with two sharp side fins coming to a sharp triangular point and large dorsal fin on its center back, I knew it to be a shark and a damn big one. *Ah fuck, Jim. What a way to go. Dinner for a fucking shark off a little known reef in a remote part of the Caribbean.*

Tobi wa by my side and I knew I would never give up the life of this woman or our life together without giving it my all. I reached down and pulled the rubber restraining loop over the hilt of my diving knife and eased it from its hard plastic scabbard. It is one fearsome knife, about 16 inches long at the blade and honed to razor sharpness.

I motioned for Tobi to switch on her light and I pointed for her to try to go past this guy on the left side. I was going to try to keep myself between the shark and her and maybe get my knife in a vital spot as soon as we were close enough. But I knew my chance of doing this was very slim. I knew they did it in the movies sometimes, but looking at this huge guy I sure didn't see how.

As we eased forward, closing the distance between us and the shark, I was able to pick out his features and I wanted to laugh. We were only a few feet from him now and I could see his slightly open mouth. He had a wide mouth and a flat head like some giant fresh water catfish. He was a shark all right. You couldn't mistake that sleek body, but he didn't have a tooth in his head, only a rough surface like course sandpaper for grinding its food.

I was staring at the largest nurse shark I had ever seen. He had apparently entered looking for his usual diet of lobster or maybe just out of curiosity. I knew him to be completely harmless and wanted to laugh. I looked at Tobi, who was still wide eyed and petrified and saw that she too had her diving knife in hand. Not as impressive as mine but she was obviously ready to do battle at my side.

I put my knife away and motioned for her to do the same and she looked at me like I had lost my mind. She made no move to replace her knife. I turned my light on the nurse shark and headed towards him. He made a flick of his tail and was past me in a blur, going deep into the cave we were just leaving.

As he went by us, the turbulence was like the vortex from a 747, and it almost flipped me head over heels. I would have lost my light if it hadn't been fastened to me.

I soon recovered and saw Tobi. She had lost her grip on her knife and it was gleaming on the smooth floor of the cave. Unfortunately, it would have to stay there for now. We were getting dangerously low on oxygen.

She was still wide eyed and wondering what in the hell was going on. I didn't waste any more time. I motioned for her to follow and made for open water outside the tunnel. We were just in front of the cave when my air gave out, and I reached down and pulled the J-valve lever to give me 10 minutes reserve.

I glanced at Tobi and she pointed up. We made for the surface not far from our launch. It was still in place, bobbing us welcome in the small sea swells.

I spit out my regulator and asked," Are you okay, Tobi?"

"I may have peed my pants, but it doesn't matter here. What in the hell happened down there?"

CHAPTER 16

I couldn't keep from laughing. Tobi was so serious and obviously still scared from the encounter with the giant shark. I said, "Come on. I'll tell you on the way back."

We made the dinghy and I laid my light over the side and slipped out of my vest with the air tank still attached. I helped Tobi slip out of hers and helped her over the side. Then I threw myself up to sit on the inflated side and slipped my power fins off.

Tobi said, "Now, what happened?"

"Well, we just played chicken with the biggest damn nurse shark I've ever seen."

"Nurse shark?" she said. "He didn't look like any nurse shark to me. He looked like Jaws' big brother."

"Well, you're close, but he doesn't have any teeth, though they do look a lot alike. This guy isn't aggressive at all and feeds on small fish and lobster and whatever he can find on the bottom that doesn't require teeth. He's like a giant catfish."

"Shit! She exclaimed. "He can scare a person to death! He doesn't have to bite them. I didn't even have to use my reserve, I just plumb quit breathing."

We laughed our relief and finally she said, "I got so much stuff to show you I am about to bust."

"And I am about to bust to see it too. But let's save it till we get back to Magic. I know the dogs are worried about us and the tide will be turning in about an hour." I pulled the little Yamaha outboard to life and Tobi worked the small bow anchor free. I headed for the channel leading us back to Port Royal Harbor and the safety of Magic.

Once aboard Magic, Tobi let the dogs out. They were very happy to see us and voiced their approval of our safe return. After a few minutes with the dogs she said, "If I keep quiet any longer I will simply bust."

She climbed out of the cockpit and sprinted up the deck. Our diving gear was still in an unruly pile on the starboard side where we had handed it up from the launch. She rummaged around in the pockets with Coco and Peanut both trying to help. She was boiling over with laughter when she was finally finished and sprinted back down the deck to where I was, holding both hands out. She stepped back down into the cockpit and opened her hands over the mahogany cocktail table in the center of the cockpit. I was awestruck as the gold coins cascaded from her hands to clunk on the hard polished surface of the table.

She said, "Surprise, surprise! Captain, do I get an 'atta girl', or what?"

I don't know which I took greater pleasure in: the proud happy look on her face, or the pile of gleaming gold coins on the table. I only sat and stared with a dumb look on my face. I had no idea she had found this large a cache, and I thought I had been watching her closely. I began to count. There were 16 coins on the table and I remembered I had put the first one she found in my vest. I ran to retrieve it and added it to the pile. 17 gold coins. We began to examine her find.

They were Spanish doubloons.

"Jesus, Tobi. Do you have any idea what you have here?"

"Well, if they aren't doubloons I'll eat my hat," she said. "How much do you think they're worth?"

"Well, they're in really good shape and I don't know exactly, but a good estimate is about $16,000 each."

"Wow!" she let out a whoop and danced a jig around the table. She gave me an exuberant hug and kiss. "How's it feel to have a rich wife?" she asked.

"Pretty damn good," I replied.

"Oh, Honey, I'm so happy I could bust. All these years we have talked and dreamed of finding something of value, but I never dreamed it would be like this. Just laying in holes in the cave. I always thought we would be in an old ship or something, finding a great chest or locker full of gold and jewels. I just never dreamed it could be like this. Let's see, 17 times 16,000 . . . Damn, Jim, that's $272,000. Over a quarter of a million dollars in less than two hours, and I bet there's lots more of these down there. How do you think they could have got there? How old are they? Do you think there's other stuff?"

"Whoa! Hold up minute. One thing at a time."

"Oh, I know, but I'm so excited."

"Me too, Baby. This is stuff dreams are made of. I still can't believe our luck."

"Well, what do you think? You always know about this stuff."

"All I can do at present is guess. But as to how they got there, I believe that's clear. If you noticed the floor and walls of the cave before it widened into our treasure room, and then again the tunnel we went in last leading on down deeper in the ocean. Remember how clean it was? Well, I think this to some degree supports my theory about these caves maybe running all the way to the Bahama Banks, or wherever. I think the water pressure going through those tunnels has swept the smaller passages clean, even smoothed the walls and floor over the ages. The pressure in the large room is less and the craggy surface has been able to trap some of the heavier thing being sucked down that tunnel, and I believe these coins were at one time on the ocean floor, maybe in front of this cave, and over the years they were sucked closer and closer to the cave like some giant vacuum cleaner cleaning the ocean floor until the current sucked them into the cave. Some were obviously trapped in the back of the cave where the current may have lost some of its force before turning and being drained through the other tunnel running off to the northeast. It's only one explanation. I'm sure there could be others. But I believe this is what could have happened."

"You don't think anyone could have hidden them in there?"

"No, I think they've been there a long time, and it would have been impossible for anyone to have penetrated that cave as we have before scuba was invented. No, Honey, I think these doubloons are probably around 350 years old. Many of them appear the same as those that were recovered from the Atocha, which sank in a fierce storm off Key West, Florida. That was in 1621. My guess is, these are about the same age, maybe even from the same treasure fleet."

"See, you don't know everything. I bet you're right, though. That has to be what happened and I bet there's lots more stuff down there."

"Well, I wouldn't be a bit surprised. I know I sure intend to find out."

"I'm looking forward to it too." She hesitated. "I am concerned about one thing, though."

"What's that?"

"That abandoned tool we saw on the floor in the cave. It makes me think someone else has been down there looking recently. What if they're still around? We could be putting ourselves in danger."

Jim thought for a minute and then answered, "Well, first of all, I didn't get a good look at it. I was too busy looking for other things and didn't pay much attention to it. So shame on me. But no matter, tool or no—it could have come into the cave the same way as the small rocks, coins, and other trash. That's only one possibility. Another is that it could have been dropped by one of the missing lobster divers of days gone by. We're pretty sure they found a few gold coins, at least the people we talked with say so. And they could have been trying to work the cave, as we have, or had some other agenda that we haven't guessed yet. Understand, this is just speculation, with very little to go on.

"I don't believe we have anything to fear from mortals just yet. But the sea and tides and undersea hazards are another story. I can't stress enough that we need to pay attention to everything, watch out for each other, and not let our good fortune blind us to the real dangers here. You are more important to me than all the treasure in the world."

"Thank you, Jim, but wow. I still can't believe this is true. How can we be so damn lucky?"

"I don't know Tobi, but I'm sure glad about it. You know, for a few minutes today I thought our luck had run out."

"Boy, me too. That damn shark scared me half to death. Maybe we should take at least one spear gun below tomorrow."

"You're probably right, but I have a feeling a spear in that size shark, one with teeth, wouldn't have helped us much."

"Me neither. He sure was a big bastard. Bet it takes lots of lobsters to fill him up, huh?"

"Yeah, that's why lobster fishermen hate the nurse shark almost as much as his more aggressive cousin. Well, Kid, you put our treasure below out of sight for now and maybe start lunch. I have lots of chores to do and it will take the compressor nearly one and a half hours to refill all four tanks."

"Okay, Captain. I won't even complain about the noise today." She headed below laughing, with both hands full of gold doubloons and her two friends at her heels.

I walked up the deck and began carrying diving gear up to the bow so I could hose it off with water from our fresh water tank. I set out the air compressor and started it up and hooked up the first tank before I began washing the salt off our diving gear.

Tobi came back on deck with an ice cold Heineken. "How about a beer? I know it should be champagne, but I don't have any, so beer will have to do."

We toasted our success over the noise of the compressor. Then we both went back to the cockpit for a few minutes and enjoyed our beer.

"How about ham and cheese and chips and more beer?"

"Sounds fine to me. You take your time and I'll finish my chores."

After lunch, we settled back in the cockpit to relax. I said, "You know, Tobi, we're going to have to keep this find a secret."

"I hadn't thought of that. Do you expect a problem with the Honduras government?"

"Only if we say something. But believe me, if they get wind of the fact that we found anything in Honduran waters, they will seize it. And that will be the last we see of it."

"Sure. You're right. So we just keep quiet."

"Okay, we agree on that. Not a word to anyone. Now, I have me a kind of sort of theory. You know, I believe the coins were sucked into that cave and I believe with the proper underwater detection gear and enough time we could find millions down there.

Understand, it's only a guess, but I think there's a good chance I'm right."

"But we don't have any detection gear, do we?"

"No, we don't. Not now at least. But I would like to return with the proper equipment in the future."

"Won't we have to be careful where we buy it? If it's in this area, people might get suspicious."

"That's true. We could go to the States and buy it there."

"You aren't going to leave here right away, are you?"

"No, of course not. Not for a while, and not until we have looked a lot harder than we have so far. But that could change if another boat should happen in here or something unforeseen happens."

"Well good," she said. "Thought for a minute I might have to mutiny on you."

"No, Honey, we aren't nearly through here yet. But I do want to try something different. I don't know how strong the current going through that cave is when the tide is running, but I think it is really strong. I believe that explains the disappearance of the divers here in the years past. Now I don't want to prove this theory bad enough to be in the water anywhere near those caves with the tide running, but what I'm getting at is this, I'm sure there would have been gold ingots on a ship carrying Spanish doubloons unless the coin was on someone's person, and I don't believe that or we would have found other denominations. So, what happened to them?"

"Okay, Captain. I give. What?"

"Well, they're either laying on the bottom somewhere near covered with sand and rock, or if the tide suction is strong enough, they're either in the cave under the sand and rock at the back wall or maybe near the mouth below the cave entrance under the sand and rock."

"So we dig," she said. "I always wanted to be a gold digger anyway."

"Right, I said. "But what I think I'll do tomorrow is take our extra air bottles down below with us besides the four we're using. We have seven scuba tanks with about 3000 psi in each. We are using four tanks for breathing. So the three extra could prove to be useful. By removing the regulator and leaving the air hose, we could open the tank slowly while holding firmly to the air hose's open end. That would create a pressure washer, so to speak, using the tank pressure to our advantage for blowing or washing sand away so we can see underneath. It would be easily handled, like a garden hose. I can turn the air valve on and blow away sand and rock. What do you think?"

"You ever do that before?" she asked.

"No, never have."

"Well, what makes you think it'll work?"

"I just think it will, but I'll have to try it to know for sure."

"Damn, Jim. You always think of everything. I bet it'll work, but I wouldn't have thought of it in a million years."

"Well, we'll give it a shot tomorrow. I'll just have lots of extra gear going out and it will take us a little longer getting to the site, but it may be worth it."

"You know I'll help. Just tell me what to do."

"No problem. I'll think some more on it tonight." We piddled around on the boat for an hour or so and decided to take the dogs ashore for an hour before sunset.

Jim had been thinking to himself more and more about the headless chicken and ring of stones they had found earlier in the unfinished marina. And he hadn't forgotten Peanut's near fatal encounter with who knows what. Maybe things had been going too smoothly and he was looking for a flaw in their Shangri-La. Or just getting spooked because things were too perfect.

As the Avon touched bottom in the shallow crater of the beach at the end of their cove, he cut the engine and bounded out to pull the dinghy ashore.

He said, "Hey, Tobi, I know you don't like borrowing trouble, but I'd like to have a better look around where we found the fire pit. I'm not sure why, but I'm curious and don't like the unknown or unexplained. So, if you want, you can keep the dogs here and I'll go nose around."

"Ha, not a chance. Where you go, I go. It's my job to keep you out of trouble, and it's probably hard to find a replacement captain around here. I'll admit I am a little nervous, but I want to look as well. We hurried away before. Not like us. So lead off, Big Guy."

We started up the beach in the direction of the old dock. This time we were staying in a tight group, the dogs close at heel instead of bounding ahead. Almost in a subdued attitude. No barking or playing this time. More duty than adventure, it seemed.

As we neared the end of the pier to climb up, the dogs were showing signs of being very nervous. Peanut had started to whine and was reluctant to go on.

Tobi said, "It's okay, guys. We're together and we won't let anything hurt you this time.

Her soft voice seemed to calm them some as we climbed up onto the dock and started into the deserted building, with me in the lead. The dogs grew more nervous, Peanut even trembling. Tobi bent down and picked him up in her arms to comfort him some as she, with Coco close at hand, stayed very close to me as I ventured deeper into the old building.

As we came up to the ring of stones around the makeshift fire pit, it was evident that it had been visited by others since we were last there. There was charred and unburned wood in the pit that was at least double the amount that had been in the ring of stones when last we were there. We were both looking around very carefully. The dogs were visibly upset. They just didn't like it there.

Tobi verbalized our feelings. "The dogs don't like it here and I feel the same. It feels like a bad place. It's in the air: the smell, just the feeling—everything. I think we should go."

"Hold on, Tobi. I feel the same, but let's have a good look while we're here."

She agreed, with reservations. "Okay, but let's make it fast."

I picked up another stick to move the trash around for a closer look. I moved the trash and accumulated debris with the stick near the back wall of the old building. I separated another headless chicken from the pile. "Looks like another sacrifice," I said. "This one is more recent and smells to high heaven."

There were other pieces of cloth that looked to be torn or crudely cut from used clothes or old cloth. Almost like quilt patches. I said softly, "Tobi, there are people meeting here, and I'm sure it's some form of voodoo or primitive worship. This is strange to us and gives us a bad feeling of unease, but we don't know that they mean us any harm. We've been thinking of this as our harbor, our place, but it's not. The people of this island have as much right here as we have. So let's get out of here and give this place a wide berth in the future. Or at least until we see some threat for sure.

Tobi said, "Me and the babies don't want to come back to this old place. Let the chicken killers have it. We'll stay on the beach or on Magic. But I had been feeling that this was our place and they were trespassing. Ah, hell. I still do. But I'll try to live with it."

We climbed down to the beach and the dogs wasted no time breaking into a run for the beach and the dinghy. We hurried as well, anxious to return to Magic.

CHAPTER 17

The sunset was beautiful that evening, shot through with all the color of the rainbow and dominated with reds and yellows. A perfect setting to end what had started as a perfect day settled in on Magic in old Port Royal. Tobi busied herself below, fixing us a special supper with her two four legged helpers at her heels, as always. Peanut seemed especially needy after his earlier ordeal.

Left on my own, I strolled forward and began rummaging in the large storage locker for our extra tanks and regulators. I found a single hose regulator and began adapting it to my purpose of blowing sand the next day. This only took a few minutes, so I laid out three extra bottles with our usual four. I had a lot of gear for the small Avon to haul, but was sure it would be up to the task.

I stored the compressor and gear we wouldn't be using and sauntered back aft and then into the pilot house, looking for something to occupy myself with. I turned on the Icom M-700 single-side band radio and tuned in an all marine weather station. There was no foul weather expected in our area for at least another 48 hours. I was relieved to hear this. Bad weather would keep us off the reef, and I sure didn't want to be cooped up aboard the boat at anchor now that we had actually found our long sought after treasure. I was bursting with impatience to be back below in our private cave.

I was still rambling around when Tobi called up from the galley that dinner was about ready and that we were eating below in the dining area tonight. I declared myself ready, my ham and cheese and chips were wearing off. I went below to the dining area midships on Magic and found Tobi had outdone herself. She had fixed a Yankee pot roast smothered with small new whole potatoes, carrots, mushrooms, and thick gravy. The wine was cooling in a bucket on the serving counter and she was looking real proud of herself, as she should be.

She said, "Well, Captain, it's not every day a girl finds a quarter mil laying around on the sea bottom, has dinner with a big handsome guy she is in love with, and then get to sleep with the captain of a beautiful yacht anchored in a remote cove in the Caribbean. I would say that's some day, huh?"

I laughed with her and said, "That wasn't an invitation for us to sleep in the master bedroom tonight, was it?"

"It sure as hell was. What do you say?"

"Well, you beat me to it. I was going to suggest it over a nightcap. But sounds great to me."

We enjoyed a perfect dinner and I began clearing things away so Tobi could have dibs on the shower to wash her long blond tresses. I had things shipshape and was just finishing the dishes when she came out of the bath turbaned in a large towel and said, "Next."

I gave her a kiss and ducked into the bath for my shower. I shaved with extra care and used some of my hoarded store of Habit Rouge Cologne in all the right places in anticipation of our night of love. I finished my toilet and came out in my towel wrap. Tobi was in the master bedroom and I could hear her dryer singing its song. I peeped through the door and saw her seated at her makeup dresser blowing out her beautiful blond hair.

She looked at me and smiled as she shut the dryer down and said, "You timed that about right."

I took her hand and led her to the large king-sized bed in the bow's master bedroom.

We awoke to a beautiful day. The rising sun was slanting into the cabin through the port side so Magic was still lying bow out to the ocean, dead in place at her anchor with the rising sun hitting us on our port side. I rolled over and gave Tobi a hug and a kiss. She said, "Let me go pee and you stay right there. I've got something I want to give you."

She returned in about five minutes and gave it to me. I was so contented and at peace with the world and my place in it that I almost hated to start the day for fear my bubble would burst. But I rolled out and went forward to the bath amidships so Tobi could have the master bath all to herself for once.

I wandered out on deck and looked around, seeing everything and nothing. Just a perfectly beautiful morning in a perfectly beautiful place. "Wow," I thought. "I don't see how things could get much better than this."

I began to uncleat the Avon and let it down to the water. I got out a spare five-gallon can of gasoline and pulled the Avon alongside and climbed down. I began filling the gas tank for the outboard engine. Magic has large diesel tanks fiber glassed under the deck dive compressor. That finished, I climbed back aboard and went forward to check over our dive gear one last time. Tobi was calling that breakfast was served and I took one last look around and headed for the pilot house and my breakfast. We decided to take our dogs to our private beach again in the morning before heading for our reef, so we teamed up on our cleaning chores to be out and on our way sooner.

Tobi and I settled down at our favorite spot on the white sand beach near the center of the crescent-shaped inner bay, and Coco and Peanut were off on business of their own. Peanut still displayed a bit of uneasiness and stuck close to his pal.

"So, have you thought anymore about how you are going to use your air blower?"

"Yeah," I replied. "I took the regulator mouthpiece off a single hose regulator already and have it screwed on an extra tank. So today when we go out I'll take six or seven tanks with us. That will give us two extra besides the two each we use for breathing. I feel pretty sure I can move a lot of sand with this rig. I just don't know how long the air will last doing this. It will just be trial and error until I see. But I'm going to take all the gear down and just attach weights to it so we won't have to keep returning to the Avon. We still won't be able to work more than two hours maximum, though, and with the tide running just before five, I still want to be well away from the reef at least an hour before that."

"Baby, do you really think the undertow in those caves is strong enough to trap a person in there? I believe the undertow pulled my gold doubloons into those holes in the cave walls but that's a lot different than a strong swimmer."

"I realize this, Tobi, and I honestly don't know. There's no way I can calculate it. But I keep thinking of all the divers who disappeared off this reef lobster diving before they decided it was haunted or bad luck or whatever and just quit diving here. There has to be some reason for their disappearance and for their bodies not being found. The only thing I can come up with is they were sucked into those holes so deep that they couldn't get out and that the bodies decomposed with time and were consumed by sea scavengers such as lobsters, or that they did surface in Bahama waters, or wherever, and were far from shore and again the sea claimed all traces."

"Well, I agree with you about your theory," she said. "I don't want to be the one to test it, but I don't really see how it can be that strong. Why do you suppose no one has come up with this theory before, Jim?"

"Well, I don't think all the drownings are known by any but the locals and it's not really so many when you think of the number of people engaged in lobster diving in these islands. The caves aren't charted or known about by many except a few locals, and they're only concerned with the tides and sea as they affect their daily lives. I probably wouldn't have come up with it myself except for those AUTEC divers losing their lives years ago and I had just vaguely remembered their little credited theory on the blue holes of the Bahamas and it just seemed to me that it might all tie in somehow, and it is an explanation of sorts. As good as pirate ghosts or sea monsters taking divers anyway."

"Well, she said. "For whatever reason, I'm glad we have this place all to ourselves. If ghosts are responsible then I even like the ghosts, just as long as they stay friendly. It's the mysterious humans that have me spooked."

"The dogs seem to have run down. Let's head back and get packed and see what you can find today."

We were back aboard Magic in a few minutes, and I started carrying all our gear back down the starboard side so it could be handed down into the small launch. Tobi made her dogs comfortable below and said her goodbyes and bid them to be good. She then secured the screen door to keep them from coming on deck alone while we were gone. She was always afraid they might playfully knock each other into the water and try to get back on the boat, which would be impossible, instead of swimming ashore, and exhausting themselves until they drowned. So she always insisted they stay below if we weren't on board.

I climbed down into the launch and Tobi started handing down all our gear. When she finished, the launch was full. I had a small clear area in front of the motor, but she had to perch atop the diving bags with her feet resting on the spare scuba tanks I was planning to use to move the sand.

CHAPTER 18

We headed away from Magic and I angled the Avon toward the channel leading out of Port Royal harbor, Tobi still perched precariously in her spot. I intended to anchor the launch in open water again in about the same place where we had been the day before. We had so much gear by this time that it was the best place to dive from, and with the sea as passive as it was, there was little problem leaving the inflatable in open water so long as it was anchored securely.

We were over the spot I wanted to anchor the launch, so I cut the engine and threw out the small Danforth anchor. I had tied four lead diving weights each on four lengths of one-fourth inch nylon rope the night before. I now tied the end of each line around the scuba tank valves so that they couldn't pull off. As I secured each line to a bright yellow scuba tank, I slipped it over the side of the launch and let it fall to the bottom. The tanks were visible from our place in the launch in the crystal clear water of the Caribbean. Next, I donned my webbed belt threaded through my diving weights, placed my power fins on my feet, and eased over the side of the launch, where I slipped my arms into my inflatable vest with the scuba tank attached to the back. Once I was ready, Tobi followed me into the water and I helped her into her vest.

"What about our spear guns?" she asked.

"I think for now we'll leave them in the launch. If time permits, I may come back for one later and spear our supper. But for now, with the extra tanks and our lights, we have all we can handle. I'll take the spare tank with the regulator hose attached to the bottom and you take the other air tank without the hose to the base of the cliff. We'll leave our lights in the launch for now and our extra air tanks will be fine here weighted to the bottom until we need them. I'd rather have the tanks for blowing sand below because I have no idea how long the air will last using them to cut sand away."

"Okay, Captain," she said. "Let's get going."

I glanced at my watch. It was just a few minutes before eleven. We headed for the bottom and retrieved two of the four tanks lying here. Holding the tank to my chest and using the large power fins to push me through the water, we were soon at the cliff's edge again. I glanced at Tobi and she nodded to me and I headed over the edge, head down, for the shelf floor in front of the underwater cave location. We came to the shelf about 20 yards or so east of the cave entrance we had been working. We turned west and were soon in front of the cave. I placed my air tank on the bottom in front of where the cave entrance was and motioned for Tobi to do the same. The wall in front of the cave was about four feet from the shelf up to the bottom of the cave entrance, but sand and small stones were sloped up to the cave floor itself.

I motioned to Tobi and pointed up. We headed back to the launch to retrieve our underwater lights. We surfaced again by the side of the launch and I reached in and pulled the large lights toward me. Tobi spit out her mouth piece and began tying her light cord to her vest. I followed suit.

She said, "I still have some more holes to explore before we try out your air bottle. Okay?"

"Sure, fine. I'll hold the light for you until you finish, then you'll have to hold your light for me. I won't be able to handle the air hose and the light myself."

"No sweat, I'm a good light holder." She smiled. "You ready, Boss?"

In answer, I replaced my breathing cup and headed back down, extending my powered light to arm's length and letting its small propeller pull me down toward the shelf at the base of the cliff on Fowler Reef. Back in front of our cave once again, I wrapped the one-fourth inch nylon cord tied to the valve on the extra scuba tank around my left wrist and looked to see if Tobi was ready to enter the fortune cave. Once again she nodded her assent and took up her regular position just on my left side and a short distance behind.

I entered the cave with the light at arm's length in front of me and trailing the scuba bottle from my left wrist so that it was up against my chest again as I switched on the powerful beam. No sign of the fierce looking nurse shark of the day before, and we penetrated the cave tunnel and headed for the back wall. At the cratered face of this wall, Tobi let her light float free on its cord and pointed to an area on her left that she hadn't been able to explore earlier. I followed her with the powerful beam of my light. She took up her former position on the wall, looking like a giant grasshopper in psychedelic dress glowing in the beam of the light.

She went from one small crater to the next. She wasn't finding any coins today, and I could feel her exasperation mounting as she flitted from hole to hole. She was up near the top of the cave to the far left when she began pulling something out. The light caught the bright unmistakable gleam of gold.

She had found a length of heavy gold chain about the diameter of her little finger. She had about three feet of the chain out of the hole when I saw her freeze. I moved in closer to see if she had a problem. She was holding in her gloved left hand a gold cross. She turned it over for me to see better. It was knotted on the heavy gold chain, which had now come all the way out of the hole. The chain was about four feet long from end to end, and, still affixed to a knot on the chain, was a gold cross that looked to be 8 to 10 inches long. Amazingly, set in the face of the cross were five emeralds nearly as large as my fingernail—one at the top, one at each arm, and two at the bottom. Also, mounted in the exact center of the cross was a blood red ruby just slightly larger. The cross was a Maltese design with heavy scrolled limbs.

Tobi was looking awestruck as I must have been myself. It was so shockingly beautiful there in this dark cave, reflecting its green and red fire in the powerful beam of the light. It was enough to take your breath away. Tobi was just lying there in the water space against the backdrop of the cave wall. She surely knew that this was surely a priceless find indeed and that all else would be an anticlimax.

Very slowly, she gathered up the chain and tried to put it in the pocket of her inflation vest. It was just too bulky. Finally, she unzipped the vest to get at the zipper of her wet suit and zipped it down and placed the cross and chain inside her wet suit below her beautiful breasts. She secured her rubber suit and nylon vest and returned slowly to the face of the cliff.

She worked the small craters on the cave wall for another 15 minutes or so and came up empty for her efforts. Finally she faced the light and held out her empty hands. She pulled her light back to herself and rejoined me.

There at the back of the cave room a lot of sand and small stones had piled up at the base of the wall. I thought this would be a good place to look first. I motioned for Tobi to activate her light and I retrieved my scuba tank with the short rubber hose attached from where I had left it on the cave floor. Letting my light float free, I rested the air bottle between my flippered feet and took the rubber hose in my right hand. I aimed it at the sandy slope at the base of the wall and opened the air valve about half a turn.

The air in the tank, at 3200 psi, came out of the end of the hose, nearly tearing it from my hand, but when it hit the wall it exploded in all directions. It almost instantly filled the cave waters with fine sandy particles. The light hit those particles but couldn't penetrate through. It only reflected back. We were both instantly blinded. It was if we didn't have a light. I was still grasping the valve atop the air tank and closed the air valve. The pressure in the hose ceased, but we were still unable to see anything.

I groped back toward Tobi and finally found her hand and pulled her to me and in the direction of the cave entrance and open water. My idea I had been so proud of and sure would work was a total failure. It was not possible to use it in the cave. We retreated from the room. The light began to be some benefit once we left the large room and entered the round cave-like tunnel leading to open water. We emerged from the cave mouth into the tranquil open water of the Caribbean.

CHAPTER 19

Back in water that the light prisms of the sun could still penetrate, Tobi doused her light and looked at me as if to say, "I told you so."

I gave her a guilty look and she shrugged. Before giving up on my idea altogether, I decided to try it again in open water. The sand and small rocks were piled up from the shelf itself to the cave entrance about four feet up the face, much the same as it had been against the back wall of the cave. I signaled for Tobi to come around behind me and I aimed the short air hose at the base of the sandy slope before the cave. I got an extra good grip on the hose this time and slowly opened the air valve on the tank.

The result was much the same as in the cave except here in open water the sand was mostly directed away from us and the light was furnished by nature from above. I was cutting away a lot of sand from the slope. The sand was hampering my visibility here also, but I wasn't totally blind. I could at least see enough to work. I kept the hose at the base of the slope, moving it back and forth and then up and back, continually moving the sand away from us and cutting farther and farther into the slope.

I kept this motion up for seven or eight minutes, only semi blind from the moving sand particles in the water, when I felt Tobi touch my shoulder. I glanced at her and she drew finger across her throat to cut the valve off. I turned the valve and cut the pressure to the hose, still watching her for a sign. She only signaled with the palms of her hands for me to hold on. We waited for a few minutes for the water to clear, then Tobi went ahead of me to the base of the slope where the air had gouged a deep trough.

She began clearing sand and small stones away with her gloved hands. I watched her intently at her labors, then caught my breath, almost afraid to breathe. I had seen the distinctive glitter of gold in that pile of sand.

Apparently, Tobi had caught the hint of a reflection through the poor visibility of the sand when she had signaled me to shut the air down. Now I joined her digging at the base of the rubble, my extra tank abandoned where it had slipped from my grasp. She had one corner exposed and this was no coin. It was a solid bar of gold.

We soon worked the bar loose from its sea grave of hundreds of years. It was a solid gold ingot, the stamp marking still clearly visible. The marking would tell us if it was cast in Peru, Panama, Mexico, or wherever.

I laid it aside and returned to the pile where Tobi was working another ingot loose. I glanced at this one in turn and laid it with the first. We worked until my air began to thin and I knew it was time to head for the spare bottle on the sea floor the next level above us. I touched Tobi and pointed up. She shrugged and reluctantly followed me up to the next level for our spare tanks.

I hovered on the bottom over our spare tanks and signaled for Tobi to stand by while I slipped out of my vest and unfastened the retaining straps holding my now nearly empty tank. I placed the new tank on the vest and secured it while drawing the last of the air from my now finished tank. I unscrewed the regulator from the tank and reattached it to my full tank and turned on the valve. *Ah, air again.* I felt great.

I then began to help Tobi out of her vest and repeated the procedure. I didn't want us both to unscrew our regulators at the same time so that if something happened—like a frozen or stubborn valve—we could share the same regulator. But at this depth, we could surface free of air if necessary. So really, just a habit. We were soon back in our vests with a whole hour of air each.

Tobi conveyed her impatience to me and we headed for the ocean floor one level below us. We worked like two beavers until we had almost destroyed the sand pile at the entrance to this cave. We now had a very impressive pile of gold ingots on the ocean floor exposed to the rays of the mid-day sun for the first time in many, many years.

I knew that we couldn't take this to the surface today as the total weight would be several hundred pounds. So before we ran out of time and air, I began looking around for a safe place to store it. I sure didn't want the tidal currents moving it around or covering it up again or even pulling it into one of the many cave mouths nearby.

I finally spotted what I was looking for. A long shallow cave in the cliff. It only penetrated the rocky face to a depth of about three feet. Perfect for my purpose. I motioned for Tobi to give a hand and I picked up a gold ingot and moved it along to the shallow cave and stored it near the back. Tobi, realizing what I was up to, followed my lead. We worked fast and steadily until we had moved our new-found treasure to its temporary resting place.

We had stored 27 gold ingots. I could only guess at their weight. I would put it around 22 to 25 pounds each, or probably near 700 pounds of pure gold. I held back away from the cliff face and looked both east and west and then up very carefully. I was marking this cave in my mind for all time. I didn't want to ever forget this location or this feeling of ecstasy.

I swam back and retrieved my air tank from the bottom where I had let it fall earlier and motioned Tobi it was time for us to head toward the surface and our launch. I had almost a sad feeling that the rest of my life would be an anti-climax after this. This is what people dream of doing for their entire life but never do. And here Tobi and I had set out on our yearly vacation, running from the rainy season back at our farm in the Rio Dulce, only half serious about our part-time hobby of hunting treasure, and stumbled into several million dollars here in this little known part of the Caribbean, the Bay Islands of Honduras.

We came up on the floor of the first plateau and paused to let our bodies adjust for a few minutes. Tobi was looking at me and I knew she was experiencing some of my feelings. After a short pause, I pointed up and we continued on to where we still had a bright yellow scuba tank full of air and two more just as bright yellow but without any air being held to the sea floor by the lead weights I had attached to them.

We broke water by the launch. It was just 20 minutes before one in the afternoon. We had changed our whole life and future here on this earth forever in just under two short hours. I pushed my spare air tank over the side of the launch and followed it with my light. I spit my mouth piece out just long enough to tell Tobi to start getting out of her things while I retrieved our three tanks off the bottom.

She gave me a negative shake and said, "You get the two empties and I'll get the full one." She pushed her light up over the side of the launch.

I knew better than to argue with her, so I shrugged agreement and cleared my regulator and headed back down. I gathered the two empty air tanks, one in each hand, and kicked myself back to the surface beside the launch. Tobi surfaced at my side and I heaved the empty tanks over the side and helped her push her full one in behind them. We stripped out of our masks and vests and threw them into the launch. I boosted Tobi up and jumped in myself. I didn't make any attempt to start the engine or heave in the small anchor. I just lay back atop all our diving gear and Tobi came over and curled up on top of me.

She said, "We must be dreaming, Jim. Things like this just don't happen to regular everyday people like us, does it?"

"I know what you mean. We always dreamed of finding something someday, something we could share with the world. But never, never in my wildest dreams did I visualize anything like this."

"How much do you guess we found today?" she asked.

"I would guess about 700 pounds of gold ingots. But without a calculator to figure ounces and the current price of gold and the like, it's hard to put a dollar figure to."

"Well, try, she said. "You always guess pretty good."

"Let's see. I would guess around five million dollars, but I could be off a few million, you know."

"Whoopee! Whoopee!" she yelled, shattering the stillness of the ocean. "Jim, do you realize we're filthy rich? You won't have to ever again get into one of those little ugly airplanes and work all day with your wheels brushing the tops of the plants and me back at the strip praying that you don't catch on an electric wire or tree limb or the engine doesn't quit under a load, or a thousand other hazards I have been dreaming most of my life. God, it's good to be rich!" She kissed me soundly.

CHAPTER 20

I spent a moment enjoying Tobi's happiness. Then I said, "We better head in. Your yelling has probably alarmed the dogs, and, besides, I had always thought we were kinda rich already. We have Magic, the farm, our business, and each other. That's pretty rich."

"Yes, Honey, but you know what I mean. Rich! Rich! Whoopee, whoopee!"

"Okay, Kid. Remember, we still have a ways to go."

"What do you mean?"

"Hell, we're still in Honduran waters and we have to get that stuff through customs in Guate."

"You know they don't pay any attention to Magic at home. Everyone knows who she belongs to and what you do for the farms there."

"I know, but they might look anyway. Especially if rumors start to fly."

"Who would start a rumor?"

"Anybody who was suspicious about our activities here. Or somebody who just wanted to cause us trouble."

I could see the light dawn on her face. "So, where do we hide it?" she asked.

"Well, once we get it back to the boat I'll lift the inspection doors going down to the keel in the main salon and just set the ingots on top of the lead keel. I can pump a little oil into the bilge. It should be enough to cover the ingots if we spread them out. I hope they'll just look like extra lead ingots for ballast atop the keel if anyone should look down there."

"I'm sure that will work fine."

"Good. Now when we get back aboard Magic I'll set out the compressor and start the tanks filling. You can change bottles for me as they fill. I want to run back out the channel and rig a mooring line over the cliff yet today."

"What's that for?"

"Tomorrow we can take a hammock down with us and load the hammock with six or seven ingots at a time. We'll tie it to the mooring line I put in place today and just pull it up to shallow water on the first shelf. Maybe three trips in the launch back to Magic and we'll have it."

"Don't you think there's lots more stuff down there, though?"

"I would guess so, but it may take lots of looking to find it. I think we shouldn't be greedy and quit while we're ahead. We have more than we need now and we still have to dispose of it, which will take some time. No, for now my judgment says quit."

"Okay, I just wanted to be sure. I *am* anxious to get home."

We pulled alongside of Magic in the launch and Tobi scrambled up the ladder to the deck. I stated handing up air bottles and our gear. I kept two spear guns, my mask and fins, and the full tank and one regulator in the launch. Then I went aboard. I got out the air compressor and checked the gas and oil. There was enough gas to fill the five empty tanks, so I pulled the motor to life.

Tobi had gone below to let her dogs out on deck and fetch us a cold drink. She was back now, coming up the deck with a cold beer in each hand, Coco and Peanut at her heels. They were glad to see me, as usual, or maybe it was just because I had brought Tobi back. But either way they voiced me an eager greeting.

I explained to Tobi that when a tank filled there was a safety pop-off valve that would go off. If she was around when the pressure gauge read 3200 psi, she should close the tank valve and attach another empty tank and open the valve on it and it would begin filling. That way she wouldn't have to kill the compressor while I was gone. It would take one hour and 40 minutes to fill all five tanks. I should return long before then. I didn't expect to be away more than an hour.

I dug around in the storage locker and came out with 150 feet coiled five-eighths inch mooring line. It was really one of four I had aboard that was required to lock through the Panama Canal. I carried this back down the deck and threw it down into the launch. I then returned to the storage area and found an extra webbed diving belt with four five-pound weights attached. I thought this would do fine to anchor the loose end of the mooring line over the cliff, so I took it to the launch and added it to my store. Tobi came along so I turned and gave her a kiss and said, "Be back soon."

"You be careful. And hurry back. Please."

"I will, Kid. No more than an hour, probably less."

I climbed down into the small Avon and pulled the Yamaha to life. I headed for the Port Royal Channel once again, anxious to get my work done and return to Tobi so we could go over the events of the day in detail. I still had a hundred questions.

#

Two black men sat hunched together in the dense jungle-like growth of the mountainside above the bay at Port Royal and watched the lone man in the small inflatable boat leaving the yacht alone and heading for the channel leading to the reef outside the bay. One adjusted the powerful binoculars without taking them off the man in the small boat.

Zep said, as if thinking to himself, "Now what that bastard up to? This first time he leave his woman behind. No place to go in that little boat but back to the reef. And why he leave her there by herself? What he do there by himself?"

The scene on the mountainside now resembled the rustic camp that it was. They had cut and trampled the underbrush to make room to lie around and move about. They had accumulated many items of a personal nature. Rumpled, dirty blankets were spread haphazardly on the ground. Dirty clothes were strewn about. Wrappers from food, water bottles, and other trash now made the nest resemble a hobo camp.

Carlos sat hunched on his blanket. His hands were busy kneading a small primitive doll he was holding. The doll was made from material that may once have been an old T-shirt and stuffed with cloth or grass. It resembled a crude human figure with arms, legs, and head, tied and sewn to give it form.

The doll had small scraps of denim sewn around the waist and made to look like shorts, and more scraps of black cloth sewn on top representing a T-shirt. The captain of the black boat? Without a doubt!

Carlos mumbled as his hands busied themselves on the doll. "You know last night we go to our place and call up the spirits to help us punish our enemies and ask for the way to punish the captain and his devil woman. The spirits tell me to make this small figure look like him and to pray and wait. They show me the way. I think I see the way now."

Zep said, "You may be right this time. I think they have found the gold coins or something big. They spend too much time on that devil reef to spear fish. And we ain't been seeing no fish. So the Powerful One send the bastard away so we can talk to his woman and take our pleasure. We know everything when he come back. If the Powerful One send him back." Zep lay the binoculars aside and stood at last.

He and Carlos looked at each other long and hard and prepared to go.

#

Once through the channel, I headed out to a spot over the first shelf. That should put me near the cave opening far beneath the sea. I moved the Avon through the water slowly until I spotted what I was looking for—a large coral formation near the edge of the shelf before the cliff face. Over this formation I cut the outboard and threw out the small anchor. I then gathered up the coil of the five-eighths inch mooring line. Finding an end of the coil, I looped it through the webbed diving belt with its attached weights. I secured them together with a large bowline knot. I examined my work, and, satisfied that the weight belt would be there until someone unfastened it, I untied the coil.

I donned my large power fins and snorkel and mask, and slipped over the side of the launch into the warm Caribbean water. Holding the loose end of the coil of rope, the one without the weight belt attached in my right hand, I headed for the bottom, letting the rope play out of the coil still in the bottom of the launch behind me.

I arrived at the small coral head and swam the rope in a circle around the head near the bottom. There I secured the circle around the rocky surface with a large slip knot so that any weight on the rope would tighten the loop. I pulled the loop tight, turned the rope loose, and kicked myself to the surface for a breath of air.

I surfaced near the launch's side, put my hands on the launch to steady myself, and took several deep breaths. I then headed back for the bottom and made an inspection of the rope where it met the rocky surface of the head. Satisfied that there were no sharp surfaces to cut the line and that it would no doubt hold several tons, I surfaced and swam over to the launch and climbed aboard. I started the outboard and maneuvered it in front of the head, securing my mooring line. I let the line play out behind the launch until I was over the dark blue water that I knew marked the depths at the face of the cliff. I took the outboard out of gear and coasted a few yards seaward. I checked the rope remaining in my coil to make sure it wasn't tangled or fouled on the gear remaining in the launch.

Satisfied, I picked up the weighted diving belt secured to the end of the line and played it over the stern of the launch, letting it fall free straight down the face of the cliff into the deep water below. I marked this spot in my mind, knowing it would be hard to spot underwater unless I knew exactly where to look. Finished with my preparations, I turned the launch back toward the channel and headed for the bay and Magic.

As I neared the yacht, I could hear the air compressor laboring to fill the diving tanks even over the noise of the outboard. I thought of Tobi's description of the compressor and smiled. It really was a noisy little bitch. I aimed for the ladder on the starboard side and cut the engine as I came alongside and stood to catch the ladder and threw my rope aboard.

I was surprised that Tobi and her dogs weren't on deck to greet me but guessed they couldn't hear my outboard over the noise of the compressor. Just as I caught the cap rail along the deck to climb up and secure the line from the Avon, I saw the white blunt bow of a fiberglass whaler. I froze in place. The white whaler was pulled in close under the sloping stern of Magic and wasn't visible unless approaching the yacht from shore or the back. It was completely hidden from view when approaching the yacht from seaward or the font quarter. I was still trying to register all this when a tall muscular black man stepped out from behind the pilothouse.

"Afternoon, Captain," he said. "You just tie that launch off on the rail there and come on board. We been entertaining your missus while you were away."

CHAPTER 21

I was deathly cold. I stood frozen in place watching the intruder on my yacht. I knew that voice though I hadn't heard it but once before. I had heard that voice on the dock at Romero's Restaurant in French Harbor in the dark early morning hours. That seemed months ago, but in reality only days had passed. It was the same voice that had threatened to kill Tobi and I with a machine gun. It was the same voice that had suddenly accused me of robbing him of his loot. It was the voice of a nightmare. How and why was he here on Magic pointing a large revolver at my head and smiling at me?

Carlos spoke. "You come on up that ladder now, Cap. 'Fore I get nervous and blow your fucking head off."

I stood mute. I climbed up the ladder like a zombie and tied the line from the Avon to the life line automatically from long habit.

He said, "Good to see you again, Cap. Hope you didn't think we were through with each other."

Where is my wife?" I asked coldly. "Have you harmed her?"

He smiled and taunted me, "Oh, not much yet, Cap. We was waitin' on you so we could have a little party."

"If you've harmed her—," I began but broke off, realizing it to be an empty threat under the circumstances. I stepped over into the cockpit to face him. He stepped back a pace and looked at me with hatred in his eyes. He was nearly of a height with me, maybe an inch or so shorter and just as muscular. I felt no fear of this man, just a cold, deep down hatred. He touched me on the chest with the cold steel barrel of the large caliber pistol, probably a .357, I registered. I still didn't waver and stared at him unflinchingly.

He said, "You be good now, Cap. My friend Zep has your missus down below in your fancy boat and he has your shiny 9mm pistol cocked and held against the back of her head. He hear any ruckus up here he blow a hole in her pretty blond head. So you be real good now. We been watchin' you since you came in here. Even see you fucking out there in the open on the back of the boat. Look like she sure fuck good, Cap."

"I want to see my wife." I kept my face expressionless.

"Sure, Cap. You just go on below and I follow you. But you remember now, you be real good or I blow a big hole in you."

I went through the pilot house door and down the steps to the main salon and froze. They had Tobi bound hand and foot with one-fourth inch nylon line they had taken from the flag locker in the pilot house. They had a long athletic sock stuffed in her mouth and tied in place with the same type cord. She had a bloody welt on the left side of her face running from her beautiful grey blue eyes as she stared her helplessness at me. I saw her small fuzzy champagne colored poodle Peanut crumpled on the salon floor like a broken doll or discarded piece of trash. Never in my entire life had I felt such a cold, blinding, deep-down hate as I was feeling now.

I said, "Where is her other dog?"

"Oh, we kill it too, Cap. Sure glad they was little dogs. They damn fierce if they big. Maybe eat us up before we get them dead."

"Untie my wife." I said quietly.

"No way, Cap. She crazy right now. We untie her we have to kill her too and then she no good for us dead. No. Sorry, Cap, but she stay all tied up."

"Take the sock out of her mouth. I want to talk to her."

"Okay, Cap. But you listen to me and you listen good. We been watching you good and we know you found a Spanish treasure on that reef. We found the gold coins you done brought up on that shelf over there." He indicated the storage shelf behind the salon divan where Tobi usually slept.

He continued. "You know that treasure belong to Honduras and its people, and we know you and that blond bitch try to steal it just like you stole all my stuff back in French Harbor."

I stared straight ahead trying to control my blinding fury. Zep, the other black man, the partner of this piece of shit with the gun at my back was standing by Tobi's side staring menacingly at me. He was shorter and huskier than the thief from French Harbor identified earlier as Carlos Soto. His color was coal black, several shades darker than Carlos. He was well muscled and had a gold tooth shining between his fat black lips. He was holding my stainless steel 9mm Smith & Wesson against Tobi's temple and the pistol was at full cock. My limbs began to tremble slightly with pent-up rage and emotion.

He gave me an icy stare and said, "Now don't be scared, white man. We not kill you or the bitch yet. You do what we say."

I repeated, "Take the sock out of her mouth."

Carlos said, "Okay, Zep. You take the sock from her mouth."

Zep used his free hand to loose the knot behind her blond head, never taking the pistol from her temple. He let the cord fall free down around her neck and jerked the sock from her mouth.

"Oh, Jim, she cried. "I'm so sorry. I was down here with the babies and I didn't hear them come aboard with the compressor running."

"Don't worry, Tobi. Are you hurt?"

"No, I'm all right. But these black bastards murdered the babies. I am so sorry, Honey. I tried to fight them and Coco and Peanut didn't quit until they killed them and this ape here hit me with a pistol on the side of my head and they had me bound hand and foot before I got my senses back. I tried to get to your pistol but they were too strong."

"Don't worry, Tobi, you did fine. They would probably have shot you if you had got your hands on the pistol."

"I don't care. At least I would have killed these slimy bastards for murdering my babies."

They both stood smirking at us and I felt the strongest urge to try for Zep's gun and kill them both, but I knew I was helpless. He would put a bullet into Tobi's brain at the slightest move from me.

I asked softly, "Okay, Carlos, you win. What do you want?"

CHAPTER 22

Carlos continued his disturbing monologue. "We ask your missus where it at before you come back. We ask her real nice too. She only scream at us, "Fuck you," and spit at us. We feel her up some and slap her around and she only scream at us that you come back and kill us both. So we finally put that sock in her mouth to make her be quiet. We didn't want her to be upsetting us. No, sir, Cap. We didn't want her to scare you off. So what you do out there on that reef by yourself just now, Cap?"

"I had left some of our equipment out there and had to go back for it," I answered.

"Why you don't bring it all first trip?" he asked.

"We had too much for the small launch and I wanted to spear a fish for supper."

"You spear any fish?" He asked.

"No, didn't see any that I could shoot easily."

"You just a dumbass white bastard in the water. Me and Zep here could shoot a dozen fish out there in half an hour. You just don't know shit in the water. Me, I dive all my life. I like a fish in the water. So now, you tell me what you find."

"We found some heavy gold bars."

"How come you don't bring 'em back with you?"

"They were too heavy and we were almost out of air. We were going to fill our tanks and go back for them this afternoon."

"Where they at down there and how come I don't see them before?"

"They're in a small cave. They were covered with sand but we cleaned the sand off and our light reflected off one and we found ten of the things."

"Maybe there be more than ten," he said eagerly.

"Maybe," I said. "But that's all I saw."

"That's why you find 'em. You got that big light that shines underwater. I ain't got no light that shines underwater or I look in the caves before myself. You ain't smart, Cap, you just lucky and had a motherfucking light. I find lots more with a light."

"Which cave they be in?" he asked. "You better know, Cap, or you no good to us."

"I have it marked, but I don't know how to tell you which one."

"How big them fucking gold bars?"

"I don't know for sure, but they weigh about 30 pounds apiece."

"That ain't nothing for Zep or me. We swim with 'em stuck up our ass. Ain't that right, Zep?"

Zep just stared his hatred in my direction and nodded. I glanced at the clock on the salon bulkhead. It was twenty minutes past two. I had the beginning of an idea in the back of my brain.

I said, "Carlos, if I show you them gold bars and the cave, you promise to let us go?"

He gave me a broad smile and said, "I swear to God, Cap. We let you go, you show us the gold."

"Okay, untie my wife and let's get started." I said.

"Oh, I don't think that be necessary. Just you and me be enou̯h. Old Zep here can keep her company while we gone. Too many of us on that ole reef, maybe somebody get lost or something. No, Cap. Just you and me be fine."

I had been secretly praying that he would say that. Tobi broke in on my thoughts almost as if she could read my mind.

"Please, please, don't show this bastard anything," She pleaded.

"It's okay, Tobi." I said.

She said, "No, it's not. You know they'll never let us go, and I would rather die here with you than have these bastards kill you and then take their pleasure on me. Please don't go."

"Trust me, Tobi. It will be all right, and, besides, I have Carlos's word that they will let us go and he even swore to God. It's evident that he's a Christian man."

"That's right, Cap. I swear before God. You hear right. So you just shut the fuck up, Bitch. The Cap plenty smart and he know he can trust ole Carlos Soto."

I glanced again at the wall mounted chronometer clock and down at Tobi, who had big tears streaming down her beautiful face. She looked at me and said, filled with emotion in a trembling voice, "My Cap, I don't have any regrets about our life together and I thank God he let me spend my years with you."

I battled back the tears that were blurring my vision and said very simply, "I love you, my darling." I turned to Carlos Soto and said, "Let's go."

He motioned me past him with the big revolver and said, "Right behind you, Cap."

I could hear Tobi crying behind me as I went up the steps to the pilot house. I said, "Carlos, you ever use scuba gear before?"

"He said. "Sure, plenty of times. I like a fish in the water."

I went up the deck and got a scuba bottle and a regulator and a pair of fins from a pile at the bow.

He said, "That tank got plenty air?"

I screwed on the regulator and opened the valve. The red hand on the psi gauge shot up to 3200 psi. "Satisfied?"

"Yeah, but you don't forget I be plenty smart. You try to trick me and you dead."

I picked up one of the powerful diving lights and headed down the deck, anxious to be away. Carlos stopped by the salon porthole and yelled down to Zep.

"Zep, you hear me?"

"Yeah," he said. "But turn that motor off before you leave. Can't hear good down here with it makin' all that racket."

Carlos motioned with his pistol for me to cut the compressor engine still laboring away. I returned and killed the motor. The quiet of the bay that had been so pleasant before was now pressing down around me like an evil force.

He said, "Zep, you hear me good now?"

"Yeah," Zep replied.

"What time that clock say, Zep?"

"Twenty-five minutes before three," Zep replied.

"Good. Carlos said "We not back here in one hour you kill that blond bitch. You hear?"

Zep said, "Be my pleasure. Carlos, you don't worry, you just get back here and tell me where that gold lie."

"Let's go," I said and climbed over the life line and down into the Avon.

Carlos said, "Why we don't take my boat? It faster."

"This is better to dive from," I answered. "You should know that, Carlos."

"Yeah, I was just seeing how smart you is, Cap." He glanced over at me in the launch. He said, "Now don't you be thinking 'bout these spear guns, Cap. They no match for this big old pistol here, and Zep, he kill your whore sure I don't come back on time."

"Don't worry, Carlos, I don't intend to leave Zep alone with her any longer than is absolutely necessary."

Carlos handed down the diving tank and light. We still had one tank and regulator in the launch from my earlier trip. Carlos still held the pistol on me as I climbed down. I pulled the small outboard to life and headed for the Port Royal Channel for the third time that day. I steered the launch over to the place where I usually anchored well away from where I had rigged the rope earlier in the afternoon. I didn't really want him to see the rope, even though I wasn't sure why just then. I glanced at my watch. It was 2:45. I knew that the tide would begin to turn any time now and would be running with force in another 15 minutes. I thought to myself, "Well, you're finally going to get the opportunity to test your theory first hand." But I also realized that I probably wouldn't be around to tell anyone about it if I was proven right, and stood a very poor chance even if I was wrong.

I knew Carlos Soto had no intention of ever letting Tobi or me leaving Port Royal alive. I wasn't fooled by his promise. I only had this deep down boiling hatred for this man who had hounded me since my arrival in the Bay Island and now two times breached the sanctuary and security of my boat, to threaten me and my wife. He had beat and mistreated the person I loved more than life itself and had brutally killed our two small companions. He now sat smugly in my launch with his stolen pistol pointed at me. I promised myself that Carlos Soto would never again see the light of day once he entered the water with me at the reef now called the Old Widow Maker. I also knew that I probably wouldn't surface again myself. But I intended to try my very best and leave the rest to fate and its gods.

Carlos broke in on my thoughts. He said, "You going in the water first and swim over there away from the boat and wait for me. I is going to cock this big spear gun and come in the water. Now, take the big light to keep your hands busy. You just remember, I be like a fish in the water and can spear far as I can see. You stay out in front of me and you do anything funny I send this here spear plumb through you."

"No problem, Carlos. I Know you're a smart fellow and I sure wouldn't do anything wrong. Not after you promised me before God that you would let me and my wife go after I show you the cave and the gold."

"That's right, Cap. I did promise."

I entered the water and slipped on my vest and air bottle. I took up the handles of the large mobile light floating half submerged nearby. This time I neglected to tie the trailing line to my vest and let it trail free. Carlos slipped into his gear like a professional and took up the powerful Sea Hornet spear gun with its five-foot stainless steel spear gleaming its lethal looking barbs from its end.

He waved the spear at me and said, "I nearly born with one of these in my hands and you no match for me in this sea. You remember that now."

"Let's go, Carlos. I understand perfectly."

I was running out of time. I turned head down in the water and extended my power light toward the bottom, helping it along with powerful kicks from my fins. I knew he could swim much faster than the light could pull me and was anxious to get below. I still wasn't sure what I was going to do, but I knew the only chance Tobi and I had was for Carlos Soto to stay at the bottom of the Caribbean.

I came to the edge of the cliff, and this time I didn't even pause. Feeling the pressure against my ear drums and my nose beginning to run from the sudden change in pressure, I continued straight for the bottom shelf like a falling rock. I glanced around at Carlos. He was as good as his word, only three feet behind me and at home in the depth. I could see his evil grimace through his mask. It dawned on me that this evil bastard was enjoying himself. He was playing cat and mouse with me, knowing this was his environment and I was no match for him. He considered me only a punky amateur in the water. I turned back to my task, heading for the cave at my best speed. I thought, "Oh, Carlos, if you could have seen me in the Navy UDT school a few years back, you just might not be so sure of yourself."

I hit the bottom shelf and leveled out about five feet above the floor and turned west toward our cave. I noticed the small cave where I had stored the ingots on my right but never paused for a second. Carlos was so intent on watching me that he had eyes only for me and didn't even give the small cave a glance. A few yards farther I could make out the tunnel-like entrance of the large cave.

I was looking for the rope I had thrown over the cliff, but I must have missed it. I had thought it to be just west of the gold stash, but I hadn't spotted it. I angled in toward the cave entrance and saw my rope lying just a few inches to the left of the opening. The brownish grey color of the weathered mooring line was all but invisible against the rocky face of the cliff. If I hadn't been looking for it, I would have missed it. I was hoping Carlos didn't see it. Again, I wasn't sure why, I just wanted it to be my secret. I didn't even pause at the cave entrance, just pulled the light trigger and continued at my best speed into the darkness of the cave.

Carlos Soto closed the distance to about two feet. He could have extended his long arms and touched me with the point of the spear. Yes, he sure was at home in the water, but he was conscious only of me. I was hoping that would be his downfall. My every sense was alert. I was feeling for signs of change in the water. I could feel the eerie stillness of the water and knew that it was slack tide, the calm period just before the tide turns and begins to run again.

I headed directly for the back wall of the cave room, and, without a pause, turned right into the tunnel leading down and northeast. I glanced at Carlos. I could feel him more than see him right on my heels. I was already farther along the tunnel than Tobi and I had explored earlier, and I could feel the pressure increasing. I couldn't see my pressure gauge without pulling the light back to me, and didn't want to pause for a second. He had to believe I knew exactly where I was going. I knew from experience that we had to be more than 100 feet down at this point and now I became aware of another sensation: a steady pressure building at my back or behind me, helping me along ever so slightly.

I knew that the tide had turned, and, if I was right, it was now running off the shallow Bahama Banks into the deep ocean and pulling hundreds of billions of gallons of water with it. I knew that if ever I was going to escape this cave it had to be now. I still had no idea how strong this undertow would be or if I could swim against it in full flow. I could only hope to surprise ole Carlos and hope he wouldn't figure things out until it was too late. I ground my teeth and said to myself, "So be it, Lord."

CHAPTER 23

I cut the light switch and at the same time gave the light a powerful push away from me toward the cave top. I arched my body toward the floor of the cave and felt a ripping, tearing, burning pain in my left side, between my left hip and rib cage. I was on the bottom of the cave floor in total darkness. I had flung myself over as I went down and could now feel the slight pressure of the tidal current on my face and shoulders. I knew I was headed back the way I had come. I could feel rather than see Carlos Soto pass above me in the total darkness. I also knew that he had made good his brag. I had the five-foot spear through my left side. I reached out my left hand and felt the barb point where it had expanded, about one foot of the spear in front of me and the rest protruding from my back. I was spitted like a fish on the spear. My whole left side was numb now, apparently from shock.

My mind was turning over rapidly. I had to get out of the cave immediately. But first I had to get rid of the spear. I felt Carlos would be in a panic hunting for me, thinking I still had the light or perhaps that there was another way out of this cave and that I knew about it. I was still hoping he hadn't thought of the possibility of the tidal current trapping him for eternity. I reached across my stomach and grasped the spear with my best grip. I took the point in my left hand and prayed that the threads were free. The spearhead turned easily and I unscrewed the spearhead, letting it fall to the cave floor. I ground my teeth harder and reached back and gave the spear a tug. It slipped easily from the hole in my side. I had to take another grip to pull it all the way through. It came free of my back with surprisingly little pain.

I knew I had no time to think about it. I had to get out of the cave or I was finished, and I wasn't going to leave Tobi at the mercy of that fucking black ape if I could help it. I gave a powerful kick, not knowing if I would run into Carlos Soto or the cave wall or what. I was totally blind. I only had the tidal current on my face to give me direction. I stayed near the bottom where I could feel the smooth bottom with my hands on my backstroke as I kicked with my giant power fins and breast stroked with my arms to gain as much speed and power as was possible. I felt a shift of pressure to my left side and it took a moment for it to register that I had probably entered the large cave room again. I turned left again so the current was again on my face and chest. I could feel the current's pressure increasing rapidly. I kicked as hard as I could. I still could see no sign of light ahead and began to wonder if I might have made a mistake after all and was going in the wrong direction.

No, I didn't think so. The pressure was less in my head and chest. I was not as deep as I was earlier when I doused the light. I kept going, but by then the current was much stronger and I began to wonder if I was making any headway or merely being swept back down the cave for all my efforts. I was beginning to tire. I hadn't swum all out like this for many years, and now I was becoming conscious of the burning pain in my side. The shocked tissue was coming back to life and screaming its protest. I kept kicking my powerful fins and stroking as hard as I could, trying to school myself not to think of the pain and the fact that my limbs that were beginning to feel like rubber.

I knew that I couldn't keep the pace up much longer, and the current was getting stronger by the minute. Then I thought I could see the water trying to change color up ahead. I was afraid my eyes were playing tricks on me or maybe I was getting ready to faint. But no, it was definitely getting lighter up ahead. It had to be the cave opening I was seeing. I tried to make myself kick harder, but I didn't seem to be getting any closer. I knew I was nearly spent, and if I slacked my efforts any at all I would never again see Tobi or Magic. I would spend eternity in this cave with Carlos Soto as my grave companion. With my last reserve of rapidly-ebbing strength, I kicked and stroked with all my might and gained the cave mouth.

The current was so strong that it nearly swept me back into the cave opening. Desperately, I kicked to my right while groping with my outstretched arms for the rope I had placed over the cliff earlier. I touched the rope where it was plastered against the cliff face, and it was nearly jerked from my hand. The tide was running full force now and I could see the sand and small stones being swept along before it to the many cave openings in the cliff face. I twisted my body against the sheer rock wall, winding the rope around my arms several times. The undertow had my feet and legs now in its grip and was trying to suck them farther into the cave with a strong steady force. If I hadn't been able to gain a hold on the rope I would have been finished.

I now had my answer to the lost divers on this reef and how the gold doubloons had come to be in the cave. I began to pull myself up hand over hand along the cliff face. The undertow was still trying to tear the fins off my feet and the regulator from my mouth. I thought, *Hurry along, Jim. You still have to help Tobi somehow before you can give up.*

I remembered my training in the UDT school and later in jump school. I had wanted to quit then too, but pride wouldn't let me. Now there was more at stake than my pride: my life and the love of my life. I pulled as hard as I could to break the force of the suction created by the undertow and billions of gallons of sea water pouring into these caves. I was finally making progress, and the higher I climbed the less pull I encountered. I was winning. I was emerging from the undertow. I pulled one last time with all my strength and saw the top of the cliff face looming above me. I pulled myself over the cliff edge. The water there was undisturbed, completely unaware of the chaos the currents were creating below. I still held to the rope for dear life and pulled myself to the coral head.

Securing the rope, I relaxed my grip at last and lay dead in the sand at the base of the coral head. I took stock of myself. I had a puckered purple hole in the left side of my stomach. There was very little blood. I knew now that the spear had missed my abdominal and thorax cavities, so it had apparently not damaged any vital organs. As for the blood, I wasn't sure. I could be losing a lot more blood inside, but at least for now I could operate. I felt like someone was holding a blowtorch against my left side. I was on fire with pain but I could handle that just as long as I could operate.

I glanced at my dive watch. It was just 12 minutes past three. It seemed like hours since I had led Carlos Soto into our underwater cave, while it had in reality been only minutes. I was well aware that Tobi was running out of time. I had about 20 to 25 minutes to come up with a plan or I knew that ape would kill her, or worse, or that maybe he already had. My hatred for that bastard Zep began to build again as I thought of all we had suffered at their hands and of Coco and Peanut whose only sin in life was their total love for Tobi.

I kicked myself off the bottom with energy I didn't think I possessed and headed for the small Avon. If that bastard spotted me, and he surely would in the silence, I was defenseless against him. I reached over the edge of the inflatable and found the other spear gun lying on the bottom. I spotted Carlos's revolver and pulled it to me. I tucked it into the waistband of my cutoff jeans. I didn't know if it would still work or not after the swim I was planning, but it just might.

I slipped out of my weight belt and let it fall to the bottom and struck out for the channel leading into Port Royal. I was only about three feet under the surface and making good time. I knew that I would be plainly visible from the deck of Magic if there was anyone on deck and looking in the water. I was gambling they would stay below until they heard the sound of the small outboard. It was a deadly gamble, but the only one I could think of. I kept kicking as hard as I could. I had my arms back along my sides and the powerful spear gun close in to my right side. I was making good time in the water and my visibility was excellent at three feet deep.

I could see the tall main mast by just glancing up and ahead. I looked at my watch. Time was running out for Tobi if this bastard followed instructions, and I had a feeling he would. I increased my efforts to the maximum. I was burning my air at a much faster rate than normal, I knew, but in a few minutes it wouldn't matter one way or another.

I finally saw the deep long keel of Magic protruding nearly seven feet down into waters of the bay below the foot wide yellow stripe that marked her water line. I went deeper then and came up under the keel, being careful not to let my tank bump against the keel. I positioned myself under the boat and eased forward. I stayed well under the belly of the yacht, my feet down toward the keel and my head looking up at her water line. I eased as far forward as I could and still be hidden from anyone above looking over the side.

I checked the spear gun and took the-safety off, extending it just slightly in front of me. Then I eased out Carlos's large revolver with my left hand. I took a firm grip on the pistol and tapped the heavy fiberglass hull on Magic about where I thought the main salon to be only inches away through the heavy fiberglass hull. I tapped three times firmly and evenly, then I lay dead still in the water, hardly breathing.

I saw or heard nothing. I waited about two minutes, but it seemed like much longer. I again tapped the hull three times, firmly and evenly. I knew this must sound like a shot in the boat salon. Again I waited, impatience eating away at my gut. I wasn't sure what to expect but wanted Zep to investigate and maybe make a mistake. At least I was hoping on top of hope to draw him away from Tobi.

Still nothing happened. I again made my three firm raps on the hull. I was looking up past the water line on the starboard side of Magic about midships, and I saw a shadow fall on the water. I knew someone was bending over the rail far enough to block the sun shining high in the western sky. I waited and held my breath. The shadow darkened and I saw the edge of Zep's head come into view. He was leaning far out, holding to the lifelines with pistol in hand, trying to see under the boat's hull.

Just a little farther, I prayed, and tightened my finger gradually on the trigger of the spear gun. I moved the tip ever so slightly to the center of Zep's forehead. He leaned over another foot and his head and neck were exposed for a second. I squeezed the trigger on the power spear gun and the spear hissed to life faster than the eyes can see.

Zep just seemed to hang there, then he toppled over head first into the bay, two feet of the spear protruding from the back of his neck and an equal amount protruding from the front. He had a dazed wild look on his face. His big black-lipped mouth was open as if to scream, his gold teeth glittering in the late afternoon sunlight. I watched him hit the water, my stainless steel pistol catching the sun rays as it fell from his lifeless grip and danced toward the floor of the bay.

I kicked myself up from under Magic's belly and took one last look at Zep. He was not going to fuck with anyone ever again, nor was he ever going to kill anyone's dogs. I tried to pull myself up the ladder but realized the tank was pulling me back. I slipped out of the vest and let it fall back into the waters of the bay. I reached down and kicked my fins off, almost passing out now from the white-hot pain in my side and from bending. I pulled myself up the ladder and onto the deck.

I made my way below, deathly afraid of what I would find.

CHAPTER 24

As I entered the salon door, I stopped and was greeted by the most welcome sight I have ever seen. Tobi was still trussed up like a pig and Zep had stuffed the sock back in her mouth and tied it firmly back in place. She was struggling fiercely to free herself until she looked up and saw me. She froze and stared at me in disbelief. Then the tears started streaming down her cheeks. I moved quickly to her side and loosed the rope from the gag. She spit the sock out like a bullet and said, "Oh God. I love you."

"And I love you, Tobi, and those bastards won't ever hurt you again. I promise."

She was talking so fast the words were spilling out over each other. I made out that, "I told that lousy bastard that you would kill him and his hero Carlos both. I taunted him till he beat me again and put that fucking sock back in my mouth."

I was on my knees now in front of Tobi working at the knots, trying to free her. She was squirming so much I finally said, "Be still so I can get you loose."

I finally worked the knots holding her hands loose and she threw her arms around me and squeezed me so tight I saw stars and almost blacked out. She saw the large stain of blood on her shorts and fresh blood running down her leg where she had pulled me against her.

"Oh, my God!" she said. "He shot you."

"Well, not exactly the way you mean it, but close. It's not too bad though, I just can't stand lots of rough handling right now."

I was fumbling with the rope at her ankle. She gently shoved me away and said, "Let me do it."

She soon freed herself and began to examine my side. She said, "They're for sure dead?"

"Yes, Baby. For sure," I said.

She only answered, "Good. I'm glad," and returned to her examination. "God, it came out your back."

"Yeah, probably lucky it did. Hate to have to carry it around the way I feel."

"Here, you set down and let me get the medical supplies." She headed aft to fetch the medical locker.

She returned and knelt in front of me and took alcohol and 4x4s and started to clean the wound, which by then was bleeding freely. I took that to be a good sign.

"What do you think we should do, Jim?" she asked.

"About what?" I answered dumbly.

"You know. Everything."

"Well, for now put some sulfa powder on these two holes in my side and 4x4s over them and then take an Ace bandage and wrap it around me pretty tight. I may need this blood another day."

She was busy at her task when she froze in place. She jumped up and started forward, toward the master bedroom. Then I heard it also. A small soft whining sound. She fell to her knees and pulled Coco from under the edge of the large bed overhand. Coco screamed with pain and I stood to go to her. Tobi turned around on her knees with tears streaming down her face and holding little Coco out in front of her. Coco was alive but obviously in a lot of pain.

Tobi held Coco out to me as if to say, "Please help her." But her emotions were too pent up to allow her to say anything. I took the little ball of fur tenderly from Tobi and began to examine her precious pet. Coco was crying also, and her left leg was stuck out at a strange angle up over her back. I felt along her spine, thinking her little back was broken. I felt very carefully until I got to her right hip. I began pressing gently but firmly with my fingers, looking for a rough bone end. The more I probed, the more Coco cried and tried to turn and nip at my fingers. I knew she must be going crazy with pain.

Tobi finally asked softly, "Her back is broken, isn't it?"

"I don't know for sure, Tobi, but I don't believe so. I think her hip is out of the socket. You help me hold her and I am going to try to rotate it around and press on the joint and see if it will slip back in. I have seen that done with shoulder injuries before."

Tobi came up from her knees and took Coco back and looked at me pleadingly. I took the small leg in my left hand and put pressure on the bone at the top near the hip joint. I rotated it down slowly and Coco screamed like a baby and tried to squirm out of Tobi's grasp. Then I felt the pressure against the leg ease and it slipped smoothly back in place. I moved it back and forth until I was sure it was not broken. Coco's sounds had dropped to a soft whimper now. I took her back and

I began to examine her again. I couldn't find any other wounds on her.

"What happened to her?" I asked. Did you see what they did to her?

"She sprang off the couch at that bastard Zep, trying to bite his face, and he batted her to the floor and kicked her as hard as he could. She went flying into the master bedroom and lay so still I was sure she had to be dead."

"Well, maybe it only knocked her out. At least if she isn't hurt bad inside. She seems all right."

She bent to examine Peanut and he had already begun to stiffen. *No miracle for our Peanut today*, I thought. Tobi let out a shudder and barely suppressed a scream. She pulled a beautiful Afghan off the couch and began to wrap Peanut in it tenderly. She picked up his small form and laid it tenderly on the couch. Turning back to me she said, "Okay, Captain, first things first. Let me finish your bandage. I'll have plenty of time to grieve later."

"I have a few things to do before it gets dark," I said.

"I'll help you," she said.

"No. For now, please, you just stay below and get the blood off the cushions where I dripped and make Coco comfortable. I'd really rather do this alone."

"You sure?" she asked.

"I'm sure," I answered.

I picked up Peanut's small form and carried it up on deck. I laid him tenderly on the stern cushions. I untied my Boston Whaler from under the stern and pulled it around by the ladder. I picked up my mask from the deck and went over the side. I swam to where my fins were floating and retrieved them. I saw my vest and tank nearby and swam to them and pulled them over to the whaler and pushed them in over the side. That done, I took three deep breaths and headed for the bottom. I saw my 9mm gleaming up at me from the sandy floor of the bay. I picked it up and placed it in the waistband of my cutoff Levi's.

I saw Zep floating a few feet away. He hadn't yet settled to the bottom to bloat before surfacing. The gleaming spear was still protruding from his neck. I went back up and took several more breaths of sweet air and dropped my pistol into the whaler, then headed back down for Zep. I was sure he didn't mind waiting. I reached out and clasped a cold black arm and dragged him to the surface. I pulled him over to the whaler and climbed in, holding Zep along the side. I reached down and unscrewed the barbed head of the spear and pulled it back through his now cold neck. The spear was still attached to a line securing it to my spear gun. I pulled that in also and laid it in the bottom of my whaler. I then began hauling Zep over the side. I felt my side screaming its protest but paid little attention and continued my grisly task.

When I had him aboard, I checked to see if my anchor was still in the whaler. Satisfied it was, I pulled the big Evinrude to life and sped for the channel and open water. I passed in front of the small Avon. It was still at anchor and bobbed its welcome as I sped by. I slowed and came to a stop over the head where I had

earlier tied the mooring line with the weight belt. I
dropped the anchor and slipped over the side. I went
head over until I had the rope. I untied the slip knot and
headed for the surface with the loose end. I climbed
back into the whaler with some difficulty now. I was
beginning to stiffen up and fatigue was taking its toll on
me.

I told myself, *Just a little more work to do, Jim, and
then you can rest.* I began pulling in the mooring line
with the weight belt attached. I hauled it in and coiled it
in the bottom of the whaler. Finally the lead belt
clunked over the launch side and I began untying the
bowline knot. This done, I bent over Zep and slipped
the belt under his still form and fastened it securely. I
hauled in my anchor and pulled the big 25 hp Evinrude
to life again and eased seaward until I saw the dark blue
water that marked the depths over the cliff face. I eased
a few feet westward until I was over our treasure cave
and took the motor out of gear. I bent forward and
threw Zep's legs and feet over the rail. I said,
"Goodbye, Zep. You go on and keep your old pal
Carlos Soto company for eternity. You cocksuckers
deserve each other."

I pushed him the rest of the way out of the whaler
and watched the weight belt pull him down into the
deep dark depth in front of the Old Widow maker. She
had just claimed two more victims.

I headed back to the Avon and pulled in her small
anchor and tied her bowline to the stern of the whaler. I
headed back for Port Royal Channel with my Avon in
tow. Tobi was out on deck watching me approach. Her

eye was beginning to blacken, but she was a beautiful sight to see as I eased alongside Magic and gave her my bowline.

She asked, "All finished?"

"All except for Peanut. I will tie the Avon off and get my trenching tool and we can take him ashore."

She didn't say anything, just stood back and let me climb up the ladder. I went to a storage locker and got out my GI trenching tool and headed back for the whaler. Tobi was by the rail with the body of Peanut still wrapped in the Afghan in her arms. I climbed down and reached up for Peanut. She handed his still form over and climbed down.

I headed for our private beach and ran the whaler ashore after lifting the outboard up. We scraped to a halt on the white sand beach where we had spent so many happy carefree hours. This time we took no pleasure in it or our surroundings. Port Royal had somehow lost its beauty in the last few hours. We headed for a small knoll at the back of the beach and I cleared a small spot and began to dig a small grave. Once we had Peanut laid to rest, we gathered stones and piled them high over the newly turned earth to keep scavengers away. I straightened up and Tobi came to me, eyes streaming tears.

She said, "I loved our little Peanut so much and he was so brave. He thought he could protect me but he was just too little and the bastards killed him for being brave and for loving me."

"I know, Tobi. I loved him too."

"Let's leave this place," she said.

"What about the gold?" I asked.

"We're leaving a friend here more precious than gold to me and the old Widow Maker has been guarding that treasure for over 300 years. Let her guard it a while longer. Oh, we may come back one day, but the memories are just too heavy now."

We headed back to Magic to make ready for the open sea, vowing to keep our memories to ourselves.

The End

CPSIA information can be obtained
at www.ICGtesting.com
Printed in the USA
FSOW01n1012201114
3531FS